CLIMB TO THE STARS

Pat's breath came unevenly.

"Perhaps I ought to apologise for that kiss."

"Ought you?"

There was provocation in her voice and in her eyes. She meant him to lose his head, and he lost it. He said:

"God! You're the most beautiful, wonderful thing in the world!"

And then she was in his arms, and for the second time he kissed her. But this time her arm crept round his neck and she was responding to his caresses in a manner which set all the fires in Pat Connel's heart ablaze and made him wonder if this was a mad dream rather than reality.

Climb to the Stars

Denise Robins

CORONET BOOKS
Hodder and Stoughton

Revised edition copyright © 1970 by Denise Robins

First published in Great Britain by
Hodder and Stoughton Limited 1935

Coronet Edition (*revised*) *1970*
Fourth impression 1980

Printed and bound in Great Britain for
Hodder and Stoughton Paperbacks,
a division of Hodder and Stoughton Ltd.,
Mill Road, Dunton Green, Sevenoaks, Kent
(Editorial Office: 47 Bedford Square, London, WC1 3DP)
by Richard Clay (The Chaucer Press), Ltd, Bungay, Suffolk

ISBN 0 340 12792 9

CHAPTER ONE

A STREAMLINE car with a black shining body drew up out-side the main entrance of the motor showrooms in Pic-cadilly. The engine ticked over noiselessly. A tall young man, almost as spick-and-span as the car, stepped out of it; soft hat set a little jauntily on a smooth head as black, as shining, as the Royale "Victor", the newest, fastest thing in cars Royale had yet marketed.

Hands in his pockets, whistling under his breath, Pat Connel entered the showroom.

Through the glass windows of an office at the far end, a girl, seated at a desk, watched the young man walk toward her; watched him smile and exchange a few words with a salesman here and there.

Jane Daunt sighed a little, shook a drop of ink from her fountain-pen, and returned to the ledger in which she had been writing. She was John Royale's personal secretary, and, as such, one of the busiest young women in London. There was no time, she told herself, in her particular life, for romance. No use sighing because Pat Connel was not only one of the most efficient salesmen in Royale's service, but he had a pair of Irish blue eyes which were too handsome for any woman's peace of mind, and a mouth which suggested that the owner liked to get his own way.

And Pat Connel meant to get his own way. He had limitless ambition. One of these days it was his intention to enter a place like this as a buyer, not a salesman. He was going to make money, to be a power instead of one of the spokes in the wheel which turned the fortunes of

John Royale, whose name could be coupled with that of Henry Ford or Sir Herbert Austin.

In the pockets of Pat Connel there was very little cash. His elegant suit, his jaunty air, were all camouflage. He worked for a salary and commission. He could adopt a beguiling manner and rhapsodise with fervour on the perfections of the Royale motor-car. At times he was sick of the whole job and there was nothing but weariness and anxiety behind his smile. But he wasn't going to let anybody know that.

Jane Daunt knew it. And she wasn't going to let him know that *she* knew. But she did, because she was in love with him, had been so for over a year, ever since he had first become one of the Royale employees.

Pat was still whistling when he entered her office. It was a blithe sound. But Jane wondered just how tired he was and how far he had travelled in that car, which he had been trying to sell to others.

"Hullo!" she said.

"'Morning, Miss Daunt."

"It was 'Jane' at the dance the other night," she reminded him.

Those very blue eyes of his looked at her with friendliness.

"Sure. . . ." His voice held the merest touch of a rich Irish brogue, no more. "And why shouldn't it be Jane now if you'd like it to be? I'm Pat to you. How's life?"

"Busy," she said. "It was a good dance, wasn't it?"

"Sure," he said again.

But while Jane remembered a waltz in the circle of his arms, when her heart had beaten much too fast, his thoughts turned to another girl who had danced at that ball, which was held annually by the firm for Royale employees. A much more important girl than Royale's secretary. John Royale's only daughter and heiress, Sonia.

6

Jane Daunt wondered suddenly if her nose was shining, and dived into her bag for a powder puff. She was glad that she had put on this new brown suit and the orange jumper with little brown leather buttons. She must have had a premonition that Pat Connel would be in town to-day.

Pat, sitting there on her desk, was hardly aware of the grace or slenderness of Jane in her tailored suit or of the attraction in her small pale face with the dark serious eyes and smooth brown head. Jane was meticulous in her work, meticulous about her personal appearance. One couldn't imagine those sleek brown waves of hair being ruffled or out of place. Nor could a man guess that there was a depth of passion in Jane Daunt which belied the tranquillity of her brows and the serene curve of her small mouth.

Pat Connel's imagination was full of the picture of Sonia Royale as he had last seen her. He had had a bet with another salesman that he would ask Miss Royale for a dance. And he had asked and got it. That was his way. He rushed in where angels feared to tread. She had treated him graciously, but with reserve, a hauteur that had annoyed and challenged him. But, God, she had looked marvellous in her shining silver dress . . . head so fair that it might almost have been silver, eyes of greenish-grey, the blackest, longest lashes he had ever seen, and a scarlet mouth which had haunted him long afterwards.

"Miss Royale looked grand that night, didn't she?" Pat Connel spoke his thoughts aloud.

Jane Daunt sat still a moment. So that was where his thoughts were! Something, perhaps her own feeling for this young man, provoked her to be sincere with him.

"Surely you aren't going to waste your time day-dreaming about Sonia?"

Pat's jaw stuck out.

7

"Why not?"

"She's the most sought-after girl in town—turning down big titles."

"Do you know her well?" asked Pat. "Tell me about her. Is she a snob?"

Jane's dark little head suddenly bent over her blotter.

"I'm too busy to enlarge on my cousin's character."

"Your *cousin!* But I had no idea . . ."

"That I was part of the family? But I am, although not many of the people here know it. The poor cousin." Jane laughed a little. "But my mother was a Royale. Both my parents died when I was seventeen, since when I've lived in the Royale household. But I insisted on working. I couldn't bear to be a dependent. So Uncle John let me train in a secretarial college, and for the last two years I've been his private secretary."

Pat looked at her with sudden interest. He admired anybody who had an independent spirit.

"Well, you may be a member of the great family, but you're not a snob, anyhow," he said. "And you've always been frightfully nice to me, too."

Her head bent low, so that he could not see the colour that rose to her cheeks.

"Why not?" Her voice was soft.

But Pat's thoughts turned to Sonia Royale again.

"How wonderful for you to live with the Royales. I think that *she* is the loveliest thing on God's earth. Tell me more about her. . . ."

But here the manager of the showrooms entered. Pat slid off the desk and stood to attention.

"What have you done this week, Connel?" The manager was a brisk business man.

Pat handed him his notes for the week.

"Sold a sports-coupé at Basingstoke—a streamline at Reading—that's all."

8

"Not bad, but not good enough."

Pat Connel, who had fought hard, using all his weapons to achieve those sales, smiled grimly.

"People want to hand over their rubbish in part exchange. It isn't easy," he said.

Said the manager:

"You're the chap to do the job when things aren't easy."

That was praise. But Pat Connel was not satisfied and never would be until he had climbed to the top. And the "top" was a long way out of the reach of a young man who hadn't a penny in the world, only one or two poor relations, and a room in Bloomsbury which was a home.

"By the way, Connel," added the manager, "Miss Royale is coming to look at that new Twenty Royale with the open green sports body. The Chief phoned from Coventry. He wants her to have it for a birthday present if she likes it. You'd better demonstrate it."

Jane Daunt looked up from her ledger and caught a glimpse of the light that sparkled in Pat's blue eyes.

"Certainly sir," he said.

"We'll go and have a look at it," said the manager.

Pat Connel picked up his hat. As he passed Jane's chair he bent over her a little.

"I'm in luck, aren't I?" he whispered.

She did not answer. She looked after his retreating figure and raised her brows.

"I wonder," she said aloud—"I wonder if any man is lucky who falls in love with my cousin Sonia."

At half-past three Sonia Royale came into the Royale showrooms. The manager was out on business. It was Pat Connel who received the Chief's daughter, and piloted her to the low green car.

Sonia Royale examined the car critically. But Pat Connel's criticism was of her.

The silver goddess of the other night was to-day an exquisite vision in a blue-and-white sports suit, a white coat, white beret set rakishly on a platinum head, white gauntlets on her hands.

"I like the look of this model," she said, and turned to him. "Let's take it out."

She was tall, and her manner was cool and superior. The touch of superiority irritated Pat Connel.

He unbuckled the strap around the bonnet of the car and displayed the engine.

"You'd like to see inside, wouldn't you?"

Sonia Royale knew nothing about the mechanism. She only knew that she liked the outside of the car because it looked very racy and very expensive. She said:

"Marvellous! Let's take it out."

"Certainly," he said.

"I'd like to try the gears," she said.

She was smiling. He could have sworn there was warmth, invitation, in the curve of that maddening scarlet mouth of hers, and yet he felt the command behind the smile, and rebelled against it. He would like to make this girl do something that *he* wanted. Of course he was crazy . . . but she had disturbed him from the moment he had first seen her and danced with her at the ball.

For years he had been too busy keeping the wolf from the door in the bitter struggle for a livelihood to think about marriage. He had flirted—his Irish temperament had led him to make love a little—lightly—in idle moments. But to-day he knew himself to be madly and unreasonably in love with the daughter of his Chief.

Later, as he steered the Twenty Royale out of the showrooms into the sunlit street, and Sonia, complacent and cool, was sitting beside him, he could smell the faint, lovely perfume which seemed a part of her. His heart seemed to beat in tune with the throb of the racing car.

"She runs sweetly, doesn't she?" murmured Sonia.

"A first-rate job," was his reply.

"Let's go to Richmond, and then I'll take over," said Sonia.

He guided the car out of the busy thoroughfare toward Richmond Park.

Sonia Royale sat back in the car, enjoying the sunlight of the April day, which was unusually warm, and the beautiful purring sound of the engine. Mr. Connel drove well, she thought. Glancing at him beneath her heavy lashes, she became more aware of the blackness of his hair and the blueness of his Irish eyes. A touch of the devil in that face, perhaps. She had thought him a good-looker at the staff ball. And she had heard her father say that Connel was one of his best salesmen. He had a charming voice, too. He was educated—a gentleman.

She found herself comparing him with the Hon. Francis Glyde. Francis had driven her down to Maidenhead yesterday. He was the son of an earl and had money to burn, and he was very much in love with her. But what a weakling he looked, and probably was, and what a bore, in comparison with this young motor-car salesman.

Something in Pat Connel's manner captured Sonia's imagination. She wished she had met him in her own social circle. They might have had some fun.

"Daddy says you're a wizard at getting people to forsake old favourites for the Royale," she said as they drove along.

"Praise indeed from the Chief," said Pat.

"It isn't easy to make people do things against their will, is it?" she said.

"No, but that's when a thing's worth doing."

"Do you always get your own way?" she asked with faint curiosity.

"I think I do."

"So do I," she said.

His heart suddenly leapt. So the hauteur, the superiority, had evaporated a little. She was becoming more human.

In Richmond Park he pulled up the car and said:

"Would you like to take the wheel now?"

She changed places with him. She put her foot on the clutch pedal. He looked down at that small foot and the slender ankle. The beauty of them made his senses swim. In a casual voice he warned her that the gear change was difficult and the acceleration very rapid.

"Oh, I know how to drive!" she said like a spoilt child.

But it only took him a minute to discover that she could not manage a car like the Twenty Royale. She would have been safer with something less responsive. He had no nerves. But he did not want, particularly, to lose his life or let her end her own violently. So he said:

"Not so fast."

Then Sonia Royale became very conscious of the young man at her side. Her lips took a mutinous curve. She was used to doing what she liked.

"I'm not going fast."

The car swerved. She slowed down a little, tried to change gear and missed it.

"Slow right down and get into neutral," he said.

"It isn't necessary."

"You'll find it is."

That carnation pink in her cheeks was lovely, he thought. She was not going to admit that she couldn't drive, and that amused him. But the fight had begun. The speedometer leapt up to fifty. Then sixty. A car came out of a side turning. Sonia swerved dangerously. Then Pat put a hand on the wheel and touched her slim gloved fingers. He was immensely thrilled by the contact, but she turned on him.

"I'm driving this car."

"You must slow down. It isn't safe, and there's a speed limit."

"I shall do what I like, Mr. Connel."

"In that case," he said, "if you'll forgive me, I'll get out and walk."

She was staggered. The insolence of it! She slowed down.

"I'll turn round and drive back," she said icily.

"Better let me take her through the traffic."

"I am driving."

"Miss Royale, for your own sake —"

"Don't be ridiculous," she snapped.

Their eyes met. His were intensely blue. To her intense astonishment he opened the door of the car and jumped out. And then, scarlet to the roots of her fair hair, Sonia put on the brakes. He took off his hat and bowed with cold courtesy.

Sonia's anger suddenly evaporated. She was immensely amused. She wondered what his reactions would be if she took a really high hand with him. A bit of an experimentalist with men was Sonia Royale. She looked him straight in the eyes.

"You're a coward as well as a cad, Mr. Connel. And you are a little ridiculous, exhibiting such fear."

That made him really angry.

He had not been afraid for himself, but for her. He wanted to prevent her from being such a little fool as to drive that car through traffic. He said through his teeth:

"Perhaps I won't take a bus back. Perhaps I'll insist on you giving me the wheel."

Sonia began to enjoy herself.

"And if I refuse?"

"I'll make it pretty difficult for you to drive."

He climbed into the car again, and with a quick movement switched off the engine, pulled out the key, and pocketed it.

Sonia said:

"You go too far. I shall see that you leave my father's employ."

Pat went white under his tan. So he was to be sacked at the whim of a spoilt child, a girl who wouldn't admit that she was in the wrong! And how lovely she was, sitting there, her strange grey-green eyes blazing at him!

"So I'm to lose my job, am I?" he said.

"I consider that you have been impertinent."

"I consider that I've been in my rights. I'm in charge of this car and responsible for you while you are in it. However, if you want to turn me out of the firm, no doubt you can manage it. And in that case, I must do something which will make me feel it worth while."

But his next gesture was unexpected, for Pat, blinded by her beauty and his own rage, caught her in his arms and kissed her on the lips.

For an instant the world seemed to rock about him. He felt exalted, ready to pay any price for that one touch of her lips. Then he sat back and said breathlessly:

"Now you're justified in getting me sacked. Go along. Drive on."

She sat stupefied, lifting one white-gloved hand to her lips. Nothing more astonishing had ever happened to her. She was furious, but she was intrigued. She managed to say:

"My father would kill you if I told him that."

"I doubt it," said Pat. "Now shall we get back? You can enjoy the thought of me searching London for a new job—minus references. That'll be difficult, but we agreed that the difficult things were the only ones worth getting."

She bent her head, hiding from him the tiny smile which lurked at the corner of her red lips. Really, he was marvellous. She got out of the car.

"Take my place and drive me home, please, Mr. Connel."

He smiled grimly and drove her home. He took it for granted that he had offended her beyond pardon and that he had lost his job. She had nothing to say to him when he left her at her home in Green Street. Quietly he raised his hat and moved away.

He was utterly and wholly in love with her now. Out of that brief, daring embrace had sprung a passion in Pat Connel that would not die easily.

But Sonia Royale watched the green racing car glitter in the sunshine and vanish round the corner with almost a thwarted look in her eyes.

He was marvellous. She had the strongest desire to see him again. He was the type of man who, having captured her, might have held her, even in marriage. But she knew, even as that thought ran through her mind, that she could not marry Patrick Connel any more than she could marry the Hon. Francis Glyde . . . or anybody else, because of that mad folly of hers in Paris two years ago.

CHAPTER TWO

GLOOMILY Pat Connel walked into Jane Daunt's office.

Jane had finished work for the day. There was a small straw hat on the side of her dark little head, and she was drawing on a pair of gloves when the young salesman appeared. She looked at him inquiringly.

"Well? Enjoyed demonstrating the Victor?"

"Immensely," he said.

Jane's dark eyes narrowed a little. Something had happened . . . she could see that without being told. She said, casually:

"How was cousin Sonia?"

"Beautiful."

"You're looking tired. I suppose it's this spring day. It's so enervating."

"Possibly. Think I'll cut along home now."

"I'm going, too."

"I've got to take a car to the works first. Shall I drop you at Green Street?"

Her heart warmed to that. It was rarely that she had an opportunity of driving with this man who was the first, the only one, to go straight to her heart.

When they were moving along in the sunshine, Pat said:

"You may not be seeing much more of me."

She gave him a quick, anxious glance.

"Why ever not?"

"I think I'm leaving the firm."

"But for heaven's sake, why?"

"I expect to get the sack."

"Pat Connel, what have you done?" She shook her head at him.

He stared ahead of him grimly.

"Made a fool of myself, little Jane Daunt. Or perhaps I haven't. Perhaps it's never foolish to have courage. Anyhow, I behaved badly because I was angry. Miss Royale will tell you all about it."

Jane's heart sank. Perhaps never until now had she realised quite how much he had grown to mean . . . this handsome Irish boy with his purposeful chin and his gay insouciance.

Living in the Royale home, she met dozens of men, rich, titled, interesting, and otherwise. Naturally, her beautiful cousin was the flaming candle which attracted the moths, and they fluttered round her wildly. But there had been one or two who had paid attention to the quiet cousin and found a greater depth and a sweeter charm in her than in Sonia. Quite recently Jane had had a proposal of marriage. Sonia had thought her mad not to accept, as it had meant money. But Jane had no intention of marrying without love. She preferred her freedom and her job in her uncle's firm.

Recently that job had become even more precious because it meant that she saw Pat Connel two or three times a week when he was not away on demonstrating tours. And if he left the firm, how would she feel about it? Pretty badly. . . .

"What on earth *have* you been doing?" she asked him.

But he avoided answering her. When he drew up before the big house in Green Street for the second time, he was smiling.

"So long. See you to-morrow . . . *perhaps*."

With many misgivings Jane Daunt walked up the wide staircase of her uncle's beautiful house and went straight to Sonia's bedroom. At this hour Sonia was generally to be found in a cocktail suit lying on her chaise-longue, resting before she changed for dinner.

And there she was, lovely, supine, fair head like silver upon a jade satin cushion, cigarette in a long holder in the corner of her mouth, fingers twirling the stem of an empty cocktail glass. She looked drowsy, luxurious. She glanced out of the corners of her eyes at the small brown figure of her cousin.

"Hullo! Isn't it muggy! It's the warmest April I've ever known in town. I shall be glad to get out of it when we go abroad next week."

Jane nodded. Then she went straight to the point.

17

"What happened during your drive with Mr. Connel this afternoon?"

At once Sonia's eyes narrowed. She put down the cocktail glass and sat up.

"He's an astounding young man."

"And how has he astounded you?"

There was more anxiety in Jane's brown eyes than was apparent in her voice.

"My dear, he got annoyed with me because I wouldn't let him drive. I admit I bungled the gears. Then he tried to order me about . . . such a masterful young man! Then I told him he was impertinent and we had a row, and I ended by telling him I was going to get him sacked."

"So that's it!" said Jane.

"More than that. Listen to this . . ."

And Sonia, who had always made her cousin a confidante, because in some queer way she respected a wisdom, a capability, in Jane she knew was lacking in herself, then told Jane exactly what had happened in Richmond Park.

There rose before Jane's eyes a vivid picture of Pat Connel taking Sonia in his arms and kissing her. Typical of him to do a daring thing like that. But it hurt her . . . jarred all her sensibilities. She wished he hadn't done it. She said:

"Are you going to have him sacked?"

"Gracious, no! I want to see a bit more of him. He interests me!"

Jane was only temporarily relieved. Her straight dark brows drew together.

"Sonia, you can't fool round with a man like Pat Connel. Surely you don't intend to."

Sonia nestled luxuriously in her cushions.

"Have a cocktail, darling, and don't look so severe. I don't suppose I'll get much opportunity to break the young man's heart. But he might break mine with those eyes of his. He *is* a good-looker! Have you got a little crush on him yourself?"

Jane got up and moved away abruptly to the window.

"I like him," she said, "and I admire his work. He takes things seriously."

"I think I should take him seriously if I saw much of him. I get so sick of the men like Francis, who scrounge round for a stray word. If Pat Connel wants a thing, he gets it, doesn't he?"

Jane swung round.

"It's bad enough for you to fool around with people like Francis, but you ought to leave employees of the firm alone, Sonia. They've got their living to earn, and in any case it isn't fair of you to lead men on. You know why!"

Sonia got off her chaise-longue and stubbed her cigarette-end in an ash-tray.

"I suppose I'm never to be allowed to forget Paris," she said in a sullen voice.

Jane turned round to her. There was nothing but pity now in her eyes.

"My poor dear . . . how *can* you forget it?"

Silence a moment between them. A silence during which they both remembered that holiday in Paris in the spring of two years ago. John Royale had sent them over because Sonia had wanted some clothes. Sonia, aged twenty-two, Jane a year younger. Yet Jane seemed much older, accompanied Sonia in the light of a chaperone because she was to be relied upon to look after the daughter who was the apple of John Royale's eye.

Those two weeks in Paris had been a nightmare for Jane. The moment she got there she was plunged into drama . . . a drama which, unknown to the family in London, Sonia had been working up for herself. She had a lover. He, too, was in Paris. And one morning, unknown to Jane, Sonia slipped out of her hotel and married him. She was secretly married . . . John Royale's daughter and heiress.

It had been a shock to Jane, and she had never dared think what effect it would have upon her uncle. Ever since Sonia's mother died, the girl had meant everything to him.

The man was half-English, half-French on his mother's side. He had a job with an English firm in Paris. He had met Sonia at a cocktail party in London. He was aged about thirty, good-looking in a rather effeminate fashion, slender, blue-eyed, and almost as fair as Sonia. He had the merest trace of a French accent, which Sonia had found fascinating. And he was an adept lover.

She had asked him to the house, and John Royale had taken a violent dislike to him. Perhaps because he realised that Maurice Gardener was a wastrel, a sponger, one of those people who manage to move on the fringe of society, and a gambler by instinct. In no way the sort of companion whom John Royale desired for his young and impressionable daughter.

In Paris, Sonia had met and married Maurice Gardener. They were to keep it secret because Sonia knew that her father disliked Maurice, and she was afraid that he might visit his wrath upon her. He was a man of strong character and he idolised her, but how could she be sure that he would not tell her to go to Maurice and let him keep her, and that he would have nothing more to do with her? Sonia was in love, but she also prized her material comforts. She did not want to give up her cars, her trips to the South of France, her dozen and one luxuries. And Maurice was always hard up, always in debt.

Jane felt nausea even now, two years later, when she recalled that moment in the Paris hotel when her cousin had confronted her with the smiling Maurice and announced her marriage.

They had sworn her to secrecy. Nobody had ever known about that marriage except herself. She had done her utmost to persuade Sonia to make a clean breast of it to her father, but she had been forced to give that up as hopeless.

Sonia's passion for her husband lasted only a few days. It had taken no longer than that for her to discover that there was another girl . . . in Paris. A French girl to whom Maurice Gardener had made promises. And Sonia had found a letter in which Maurice protested undying passion for this Colette, who was a mannequin, and stated that he was marrying Sonia Royale entirely for her money.

Then there were scenes, reproaches, attempted explanations on the part of Maurice, and finally Sonia, her passion spent and dead, returned to London with her cousin—alone. Never again would she live with Maurice. Both she and Jane extracted from him an oath that he would not appear in England or interfere in her life, and in return Sonia would send him money when she could. So far, he had kept his promise. He had not worried her at all, and part of her allowance went to Paris regularly to keep him quiet.

That secret hung heavily upon Jane's conscience. She never thought of Maurice Gardener without wishing to God that she could make a clean breast of the marriage to her uncle. To-day, she said:

"Isn't it time you made some effort to get a divorce from Maurice? Why not rely on your father's devotion to you and let him help you out of this mess, so that you can think about marrying somebody else if you want to."

Sonia turned on her with the usual protest.

"I shall never tell father. I won't risk it. I couldn't bear to be thrown out and made to go to *him*."

So Jane, with the thought of Pat Connel uppermost in her mind, said:

"Then you must leave other men alone."

And that was the conclusion, with only one satisfaction for Jane. She learned from Sonia that Pat Connel was not to be dismissed from the firm.

CHAPTER THREE

NOBODY was more astonished than Pat Connel when his expected notice to "quit" failed to come. He was fully prepared for it. But nothing happened. The manager saw him that next morning and sent him on one of his usual trips down to the West Country to demonstrate a Twenty Royale.

Pat saw Jane Daunt for a few minutes before he set off. He was touched when she said:

"So you're off on business! There was nothing in that sinister remark of yours about leaving the firm? I'm so glad."

She had seemed glad. He liked little Jane Daunt. She would make a grand friend. And somehow he never connected her with the Royales, never felt that it was an impertinence to call her by her Christian name or treat her like a pal. Certainly she bore not the slightest resemblance to Sonia.

He did not see Sonia again until a week later, when he was driving one of the Royale saloons down Piccadilly. He was held up by a red signal and found himself alongside a big grey-and-silver Royale Victor which he knew at once belonged to the head of the firm.

The Chief, a grey-haired man with a rosy complexion and small twinkling eyes, was driving the car, and his daughter sat beside him. Pat Connel's heart raced. He stared in Sonia's direction. She turned her head and recognised him. She was lovely, he thought, in grey, toning with the car and wearing a chic mink cape, for there was a cold wind and the April day was not so warm.

He fancied that her cheeks reddened when she caught his eye, and he could have sworn that a smile lurked at the corner of her mouth, and there was direct challenge in the gaze she turned on him. Then the green lights flashed. They moved on and Pat lost sight of father and daughter in the big grey car.

Sudden depression seized him. He was a fool to feel this way about Sonia Royale. Obviously she was out of his reach. And yet, hadn't he refused a dozen times in his life to admit that anything was beyond the reach of a man who had the courage of his convictions and lived by them?

Sonia said to her father:

"That was one of our cars. Did you see it?"

"Yes, with young Connel."

"Do you like Mr. Connel?"

"First-rate salesman and an educated fellow into the bargain. Yes, I like him," was John Royale's reply.

Sonia shut her eyes and thought of a hot kiss which had been laid upon her lips and of Pat's Irish blue eyes burning down into her own. She must see him again. She didn't care what Jane had to say!

Later that day the London manager told Pat Connel that the Chief was going abroad. He was taking his daughter and his niece with him; the latter as his secretary. John Royale, apart from his business, was writing a book of travel for a hobby. Sonia had the fun of the trip, and Jane took down the notes and did the work.

"Connel, you're to take the grey saloon up to the works and get her overhauled," said the manager. "They're taking her through France, and possibly Spain."

"Is the Chief driving himself?" asked Pat.

"No, they're taking Woodham, their chauffeur."

Pat considered this gloomily. It meant that Sonia Royale would be away for weeks. He would have to just picture her being driven those hundreds of miles into the heart of Spain and North Africa, which would be enchanting now, perfect in the spring. Pat knew Morocco. In better days, when he was on holiday from school, he had gone to Tangier with his father.

Why couldn't he go now? Why must he stay behind just selling cars—selling cars—nothing else? As he took the big saloon out to the service depôt at Wembley, an overwhelming desire to accompany Sonia Royale on that trip seized him. It was, on the face of it, a desire as ridiculous and hopeless as the rest. But that night Pat's wild streak was uppermost.

He did not go straight back to his room in Blooms-bury that evening. He called at some Mews just behind the Royale house in Green Street, where Woodham, the chauffeur, lived with his wife and two children. Pat knew Woodham well. They had come up against each other on the question of cars and respected each other.

He found the chauffeur sitting in the kitchen with his eldest child on his lap, shirt-sleeves rolled up, pipe in his mouth. He had just finished washing down Miss Royale's green racer.

He greeted Pat pleasantly.

"I want to talk to you, Woodham," said Pat.

The chauffeur sent his small boy out of the kitchen.

"Anything I can do, Mr. Connel?"

Pat lit a cigarette and eyed the chauffeur through the smoke.

"Are you keen about this trip to Morocco?"

Woodham's face became downcast.

"Far from it, Mr. Connel. It's orders from headquarters and all that, but I never did care for foreign parts, and there's a lot of reason why I don't want to go just now. The missus is only just out of hospital, and not picking up very fast. She's fretting her heart out about me going abroad."

Pat bit his lip. He was sorry for Woodham, but the news was good from his own point of view. He sat talking to Woodham. Next Monday, Woodham was to take the car over to Dieppe on the night-boat. The others intended to fly to Paris the previous day, because the Chief had a business deal there, and the following morning were taking the train down to the coast, where they would meet Woodham and the car.

"Things ain't easy, Mr. Connel," the chauffeur finished. "But I don't see as how I can refuse to go without getting the sack."

Pat had a sudden vision of Sonia Royale in his arms, that provocative mouth of hers quivering under his.

"You're right," he said. "Things aren't at all easy. But I've got a proposition to make to you. If you like to agree to it, things might be less difficult for both of us."

The chauffeur took the pipe from his mouth and stared.

"How's that, Mr. Connel?"

"Look here, I saved twenty-five quid last year. Supposing you have it and take your wife away to the sea for a holiday, and *I* take the car over to Dieppe on Monday."

Woodham stared harder, then laughed.

"You're joking, Mr. Connel."

But Pat talked to him hard for ten minutes and managed to convince him that it was far from a joke.

"You're not going to lose your job," he finished, "and I shall tell the Chief when I get the other side, that your wife was taken bad and you couldn't leave her. So I, having heard about it, offered to go in your place. You know how nervy he is about being driven by anybody but you, so a new chauffeur would cause the dickens of a fuss. But I've driven him, and he trusts me."

"But Mr. Connel—'

"Let me finish. I can-wear your uniform—we're the same height. And added to that, I happen to speak Spanish, because when my father was alive I was going to have a job in South America, and I learned the language. Then it all fell through, and so I became a salesman for Royale. But the Royale family will find me pretty useful in Morocco, and you'd like to take the wife to the sea, wouldn't you, Woodham?"

The chauffeur's honest face worked.

'By gum, I would, but it don't seem hardly right."

"On the other hand, it isn't very wrong, and if you'll leave it to me—'

"But what on earth do you want to do a chauffeur's job for, Mr. Connel?"

"Ah!" said Pat, and thought of a platinum head and a pair of challenging green eyes. "Now, what about it, Woodham? Are you on?"

A moment's hesitation. From upstairs came a baby's wail and the sound of a woman's tired voice. Twenty-five pounds to spend on a holiday, and Maggie ailing, badly in need of it. Woodham squirmed.

"Gawd! It ain't easy to turn that down."

Pat's slim brown hand shot out and the chauffeur's horny fingers closed over it.

CHAPTER FOUR

ONE week later, John Royale, his daughter Sonia, and Jane Daunt were driven by Woodham to Croydon Aerodrome, where they boarded an Imperial Airways liner for Paris.

But it was not Woodham who drove the big grey saloon with the gleaming silver bonnet down to Newhaven and got on board the night-boat for Dieppe. It was Pat Connel. And now he stood on deck in the April starlight, looked across the rippling onyx water and thrilled at the prospect of meeting Sonia at the other side. He had left a note for the manager in London, telling him that he had been ordered abroad at the last moment with the Chief. It was an immense piece of cheek on his part, and he knew it. But the story he had ready for the Chief was watertight.

He was staking a lot on this, and he knew it. But wasn't it worth while? The possibility of six glorious weeks on the Continent beside *her*.

Little Jane Daunt would open her eyes wide when she saw him. She had taken special pains to say good-bye to him last night before she left the office. He had almost fancied that she was reluctant to say it. She was awfully nice to him, and he liked her. He wondered if there was some fellow that she cared about and if things were as difficult for her as for himself? She rather gave one that impression. There was always something a little wistful in those dark eyes of hers. But it never entered Pat Connel's head to associate that look with himself.

He slept soundly on board that night, and took the car off at Dieppe at eight o'clock the next morning.

At midday he was at the station to meet the boat-train from Paris.

A pulse beat rather thickly in Pat Connel's throat when he saw the Royale party descend from the train. Now for the fireworks, if any. There was Jane . . . the first to descend . . . neat and small in a tweed travelling coat and a beret. And then Sonia. His heart thrilled to the sight of her beauty. She was a peerless girl, wonderful in that silky mink coat, and a tiny green hat with a little lace veil across her eyes. Then finally John Royale directing porters and baggage.

Jane was the first to spot Pat. For a moment she thought her eyesight was playing tricks with her. It was Woodham who was expected to meet the train. But it wasn't Woodham who stood there in that olive-green uniform with the polished buttons, black glossy leggings, and a peaked cap at rakish angle on a handsome head. *That was Pat Connel.* As he neared her, he caught her eye and grinned like a truant schoolboy.

"Good heavens alive!" said Jane.

Then Sonia saw Pat. She, too, uttered an exclamation.

"Good lord!"

Pat Connel approached the Chief and touched his cap. He said in a clear voice:

"I have to report, sir, that I have come in Woodham's place. Woodham's wife was taken ill at the last moment and it was not advisable for him to leave her. He didn't want to let you down, so knowing how you dislike strange chauffeurs, I volunteered to come, and hope you don't mind, sir."

John Royale was surprised and a little put out. It had never entered his head that Woodham would not come, and it was somewhat disconcerting to find one of his salesmen in the chauffeur's place. He knew, however, that young Connel was an excellent driver, and, of course, an educated fellow. It wouldn't be unpleasant to have him on the tour. Pat made haste to add that he could speak a little Spanish.

"Well, well," said John Royale, "that'll be pretty useful. And if you don't mind the job, Connel, of course come along with us by all means."

He spoke in the kindly manner which endeared him to all his employees. There was no nicer man than John Royale. But Jane Daunt, her small mouth tightly closed, looked at Pat and entertained the serious suspicion that this was not all "on the level". She knew Pat only too well. She would not put it past him to have engineered this business. And if he had, and all for the sake of being with Sonia, then he was mad. And it would be a mad trip for all of them.

Pat was not looking at Jane. He was looking at Sonia. He moved forward and took a small suitcase out of her hand.

"Allow me, miss," he said.

Sonia looked straight up into his eyes and saw the devil lurking in them. He was amazingly attractive in that uniform. He looked more like a young Spanish officer than a chauffeur, she thought. She did not wonder how or why he had come. She merely knew that she was entranced to have him during this holiday. She had expected to be bored with just her father and her cousin. Pat Connel's company was worth having.

As Pat turned away to conduct them to the car, Sonia whispered to Jane:

"I say, what awful fun!"

Jane said stonily:

"Is it?"

"More than that, Jane. Do you know, I believe I'm really smitten with your Mr. Connel?"

Her Mr. Connel. How far from the truth that was!

Jane looked at the back of the tall, graceful figure in the green uniform and clenched her small teeth.

"You fool, Pat Connel," she thought. "*You fool* to have done this."

The luggage was strapped on to the car. They were all travelling very light and had taken as little as possible.

Pat's heart sang as he took his place at the wheel. The gamble had come off! Everything was set fair for a marvellous time. The Chief had accepted him, and Sonia's wonderful eyes had even welcomed him . . . only little Jane Daunt looked as though she wasn't pleased. He couldn't think why.

"You'd better sit with Connel, Babe," John Royale addressed his daughter. "Jane and I will sit at the back, because I want her to take some notes on the scenery as we drive along."

And that was the way they set off down the straight road which led out of Dieppe toward Rouen. Sonia, warm and luxurious in her furs under a Jaeger rug, sat beside Pat—near—so near to him that he could detect that familiar heady perfume of hers. And his heart exulted at her nearness and the friendliness with which she now talked to him about the trip as they moved along. She appeared to have forgiven him completely for that kiss the other day. But he knew she could not have forgotten it, any more than he had done.

And Jane, trying hard not to feel absurdly jealous and honest anxiety for Pat, jotted down in shorthand the remarks which her uncle made about the route which they traversed.

Every now and then Jane's brown eyes lifted from her notebook, and she could see Sonia's fair head with its impudent little hat, leaning closer and closer to the shoulder of the handsome driver. How could she! It made

Jane writhe . . . how could she flirt like this, knowing Pat's position . . . knowing her own?

It was a lovely day in spring. The French countryside was looking its best. They passed through Rouen and Evereux and by nightfall were at Chartres, where they were to end the first day's journey. John Royale wanted photographs and notes on the cathedral there, which was the second most perfect example of Gothic architecture in France.

It was when they arrived at the Hôtel de Ville that Jane felt most unhappy about Pat. For, of course, there was no question of his being "one of the party". John Royale took a handsome suite for his daughter and his niece, and Pat went to the chauffeur's quarters.

There was one awkward moment when Pat carried some of the luggage into the vestibule of the hotel. Sonia, having thoroughly enjoyed her journey and knowing full well what effect she had had upon Pat because she had chosen to be charming, whispered to her father:

"He isn't like Woodham, Dad. . . . Don't you think he ought to have a better room? . . . I mean, not be boarded like a servant. . . ."

John Royale agreed. On the other hand, he found the situation a little embarrassing. But it was Pat himself who put an end to it.

"I've come in Woodham's place, and I must be treated as Woodham," he announced. "I shall be perfectly happy. I shall wash down the car and be at your disposal in the morning, sir."

Jane did not know whether to be glad or sorry. But she lingered a moment by the car when Pat took his seat to drive round to the garage. Their gaze met. His smiling eyes were almost defiant. He could read disapproval in hers.

"Anything I can do, miss?"

"Pat Connel, you're a very unscrupulous young man," said Jane severely. "Drop this chauffeur business and tell me the truth. Was Woodham's wife so seriously ill that he couldn't come?"

"That's what I said."

"But it's not what I believe."

"You aren't trying to suggest that I manœuvred this, are you?" His smile mocked her.

"It was wrong. You've no right to be here, and it will only lead to trouble."

"Why should it? The Chief is very amiable, and *She* was angelic all day. I was half afraid she'd be so furious with me that she'd get me the sack on the spot."

"I almost wish she would," said Jane under her breath.

Then Pat ceased smiling.

"Don't damp my spirits, Jane. Can you blame me for wanting to be near her? It may be awful cheek on my part to even think about her, but I can't help it."

Jane stood motionless, the cool night wind blowing against her face. Her gaze turned from the serious, attractive face of the young Irishman to the glittering lights of the hotel wherein Sonia waited for her to come and help unpack . . . if not to do most of the unpacking. She felt wretched and helpless.

"It's a nice situation," she told herself gloomily, "to watch the man I'm in love with walking straight over a precipice, and not be able to pull him back."

Pat switched on the engine.

"You seem scared to death of me falling for your lovely cousin," he said. "But don't be. I can take care of myself, you know. Good night, little Jane Daunt."

Then he was gone, and she was left staring after the car helplessly.

Some hours later a slim, elegant girl in a white fur coat stole out of the Hôtel de Ville and stepped into a grey-and-silver car which was drawn up at the entrance. Immediately the door was shut and the car moved away.

Sonia Royale loosened a big white fox collar, revealing a white throat and a glimpse of black velvet and pearls, and gave a little laugh as she stretched slim ankles in tiny high-heeled shoes before her.

"What a marvellous night for a drive," she murmured.

Pat Connel nodded, but said nothing. Nobody had been more surprised than himself when an order had been sent to the servants' quarters that he was to take the car round to the front entrance at nine o'clock.

Having spent an hour washing down the mud-splashed body, which was no light job, and one to which he was not accustomed, Pat had felt tired and ready for bed. He had not bargained for night as well as day work. But all feelings of fatigue or resentment vanished the moment he saw that it was Miss Royale who wanted the car, and that she came alone.

There was magic in the night now, and in the presence of this bewitchingly lovely young woman who sat beside him.

"Where do you want to go?" he asked.

"Nowhere in particular. Just drive a little way out and then stop. I must get some fresh air. It's so stuffy in these over-heated hotels. Daddy's immersed in writing, and I told him I was going to bed, and Cousin Jane is typing out her notes. She's very conscientious."

"I like Miss Daunt," said Pat. "I think she's a fine girl."

Sonia made a little moué with her curved red lips.

"Oh, yes—she's a dear. But, of course, it's a little boring sometimes to have a relation like that perpetually with one."

The cattiness in that remark escaped the young man, who was so blindly enamoured. He said:

"Lucky relation to be near *you*—*perpetually*."

"The Irish have a wonderful faculty for saying nice things. Drive faster," said Sonia.

Gravely Pat touched his peaked cap.

"Yes, miss."

"Don't call me that. You're not Woodham."

Jane had said that to him a few hours earlier, and it had merely amused him. But from Sonia it sounded different . . . it made his blood leap.

"You're very nice to me, Miss Royale."

"Do you know that my cousin Jane thinks that you did this on purpose . . . that Woodham's wife isn't so ill . . . in other words, that you engineered the whole thing?"

Pat squared his chin and looked ahead.

"That's a very serious allegation."

"I wouldn't put it past you, Pat Connel. You're rather an outrageous young man," said Sonia softly.

The red blood warmed his brown face.

"Am I?"

"*Was* this a plot?"

He did not answer. But she saw a smile lurking at the corner of his well-shaped mouth, and a warm little glow came over her as she remembered how those lips had claimed hers—in Richmond Park.

"Tell me," she said. "Come along . . . why keep the truth from me?"

"Very well. I did engineer it. I wanted to come, and it was the only way I could manage it."

"It was a very clever way. What did Woodham say about it?"

"He was a bit scared. You'll never, never blame him, will you?"

Sonia stifled a laugh.

"No; you're obviously the culprit. Did you bribe him?"

"Yes."

"Money to burn—eh?"

"Far from it. But it was worth everything I had to get out here."

Sonia thrilled. Her vanity was wholly satisfied by the thought of this impecunious young man throwing away his last penny in the effort to be near her. Of course it *was* that.

"Why were you so terribly anxious to join this party?" she asked him.

He wondered, suddenly, if this lovely girl, heiress to a fortune, was merely fooling with him. He froze at the thought. Abruptly he drew the car in to the side of the road, which was dark and lonely and a little way out of the town. The sky was brilliant with stars, but there was no moon, so he could not see more than the dim outline of her face. There was a rough note to his voice when he spoke again.

"I don't know why you want to know all these things, Miss Royale. I don't know why you should be interested —but if you want the truth—here it is. I came because I wanted to be near you. That may be an impertinence, but I'm not ashamed of saying it."

Sonia drew in a deep breath. She was nearer in that instant to feeling real sincere emotion than she had ever been in her life before. There was something about this forceful, impetuous young man which appealed to the feminine in her, bred in her a wholly feminine desire to conquer him utterly. He was the kind that would be worth conquering. It was partly her insatiable vanity and partly a desire for closer contact with him that led her to forget that she was not free and had no right to offer him even an instant's encouragement. She knew full well that whatever Pat Connel did would be in deadly earnest.

She leaned a little nearer him until a strand of her silver-fair hair touched his chin.

"You needn't be ashamed of saying anything—to me.

And why shouldn't I be interested? Why shouldn't I be even flattered because you took so much trouble to come out here and be with me?"

"You can't mean that," he said.

But she put out a hand and felt for his. He crushed it in a grip that made her wince. She could feel his fingers shaking.

"And why do you think I didn't report you to my father when you behaved so badly in London?"

Pat's breath came unevenly.

"I consider *you* behaved rather badly too."

"Perhaps I realised that."

"And perhaps I ought to apologise for that kiss."

"Ought you?"

There was provocation in her voice and in her eyes. She meant him to lose his head, and he lost it. He said:

"God! You're the most beautiful, wonderful thing in the world!"

And then she was in his arms, and for the second time he kissed her. But this time her arm crept round his neck and she was responding to his caresses in a manner which set all the fires in Pat Connel's heart ablaze and made him wonder if this was a mad dream rather than reality.

CHAPTER FIVE

THE glamour of that starlit spring night on the Chartres road, and the warmth and beauty of Sonia in his arms, cast a spell upon Pat Connel which rendered him incapable of using his brain at all.

A little sane thought and he might have asked himself what possible wisdom lay in, plunging into a hotly passionate love affair with the daughter of his Chief. He might have doubted his sanity in allowing himself to be so completely enslaved by the witchery of this girl. For although he was very man to her woman while his arms were about her and his lips against her mouth, nothing could alter the fact that he was an impecunious employee in her father's firm, and that she was heiress to a fortune.

He could be neither wise nor sane while her heart beat to the same mad glad tune as his. He could only whisper between his kisses:

"I love you ... I love you ... you know that I do!"

Sonia found herself slipping into an enchanted world. She had not meant to. She had wanted to be practical about this affair, and never for an instant to lose sight of the difference in their stations. But Pat was an ardent and charming lover, and his obvious adoration was most flattering. Added to which she was genuinely attracted by him. While she rested languorously in his embrace, her eyes shut, her fingers caressing the thickness of his black handsome head, she genuinely wished that she had met and loved him under very different circumstances to these.

"You're so lovely ... you're like a flower ... an angel ..." Pat's husky Irish voice was pouring endearments into her ear.

The longer she listened and the closer she clung to him, the more sincerely did Sonia regret the impossibility of this situation. But she was too much of an egotist to allow herself to be conscience-stricken for long. Jane, of course, would tell her that she had no right to behave like this. Jane would say that it was grossly unfair to Pat Connel. Perhaps it was. He seemed so grave about it all. She sighed, and whispered:

"Oh, Pat!"

Then his arms slackened and he drew slightly back from her. His eyes probed deeply into hers.

"Why . . . why are you like this? Why are you being so sweet, so kind to me? I don't understand."

She smiled.

"Don't try. Put your arms around me again."

"But I must know. I want to understand. I've had the most colossal nerve, making love to you like this. . . ."

"Thank goodness you have."

"You wanted me to?"

"Isn't that obvious?"

"But, Sonia . . ." For the first time he was using her Christian name. His brain was hazy. He was like one drunk with love. "It's unbelievable . . . that you should feel like this about me."

"I'm not the first woman to feel like this about you, Pat. You've got the devil in your eyes, and you know it."

"But, Sonia . . ." He stammered wildly, caught her other hand in his and kissed it. "You're so lovely, so wonderful."

She leaned toward him, sighing luxuriously.

"Am I!"

"Marvellous! . . . I could never tell you how marvellous! And I can't quite get accustomed to the thought that you want me to make love to you. . . ."

"Certainly I want you to."

"Do you love me?"

"Can't you guess?"

"But do you, *do you?*"

"Yes." She whispered the word with her lips against his ear. And again he kissed her with a passion that blinded her temporarily to everything on earth but the power of his personality and the sheer attractiveness of him as a lover.

His ardour moved her, called forth as much sincerity of feeling as she was capable of for any man. But she was frightened of that feeling. She did not want to love Pat

Connel too much, otherwise she must necessarily think of his happiness before her own. And then she must inevitably end this affair speedily before it hurt him too much. There was nothing light or philandering about this young man's love for her. She knew it. It burned with a white-hot sincerity.

Now she drew away from him. She said:

"My sweet, we must be sensible."

He took a deep breath, like a man who has felt himself drowning and comes up to the surface again. He kept her hands fast in his.

"I adore you. You know that now, don't you?"

"Yes."

"I've always adored you. I fell in love with you that night at the ball when I first danced with you and you were so proud and aloof. You were just John Royale's daughter and heiress that night, being condescending to one of the lesser lights in the firm."

She laughed.

"That sounds awful. Was I so horrid?"

"You were wonderful. You always are."

"Even when I insisted on driving a car that I couldn't drive?"

"You were grand. That day at Richmond I fell more in love with you than ever."

"You were awfully daring, weren't you, my sweet? I might quite easily have had you turned out of the firm for kissing me."

"I don't know why you didn't. I expected you to."

"You know now why I didn't."

His heart beat hard and fast.

"Sonia, don't fool with me, will you? Don't lead me to believe that you were kind to me because you fell in love with me . . . unless it's true."

Her fingers stirred a trifle restlessly in his.

"It's quite true."

"But why . . . why . . .?"

"You're not going to ask questions all over again, are you? Hush, my sweet . . . don't try to analyse it. Just be happy like I am."

"But I must analyse it. It's so frightfully important. Don't you see what it means? It might be the beginning . . . or the end of everything."

"That sounds cryptic!"

"But you must try and understand what I feel. I'm madly, desperately in love with you. For some reason which I shall never understand, you're being an angel to me and trying to make me believe that you love me too. Well, that *is* the beginning and the end of the world so far as I'm concerned."

"Why the end?"

"Just that there can never be anybody else but you."

A shadow crossed her face, but in the dim starlight he did not see it. She drew her hands away from his, found a flapjack in her evening bag, and automatically dusted her face with powder . . . a face that burned from Pat's impassioned kisses.

He went on speaking:

"I once had the impertinence to wonder whether I could ever make you love me. . . . I dreamed wild, impossible dreams about you. Yet now you're making them possible, and that's what makes my brain quite dizzy. It's too good to be true."

"Darling," she murmured, and wished for the first time in her life that she was not John Royale's heiress, but quite a poor, unknown girl who could have married this man.

"But you see," continued Pat, "now that you are making my dreams come true, I'm full of doubts and fears."

"About what?"

"Not about my love for you. That's indubitable. But about the future. What possible right have I got to propose marriage to you?"

Sonia frowned. She did not like that word "marriage". It made her feel much too uncomfortable. It reminded her much too painfully of the fact that she was not free to listen to a proposal from any man.

"Don't let's worry to-night about the future," she said in a low voice.

"But I must. I love you and I want to marry you. It may sound wildly impudent . . . for me to propose to you . . . but if you care for me . . . Sonia, darling, there isn't anything in the world I wouldn't do to try and win you. That look in your eyes just now when I kissed you . . . my God, that's sufficient to spur any man on to the most incredible victories. I feel I could scale mountains . . . swim oceans . . . conquer worlds. . . ."

"You say such marvellous things, my sweet."

"But I mean them. Only tell me that you love me and that you want to marry me, Sonia, and I'll start right now making myself worthy of you."

Sonia swallowed hard. For a little while she had been caught up in Pat's whirlwind of ardour and carried along despite herself. But now he was rushing beyond her. She could not, *must not* follow him. She said:

"Not so fast, darling, *please*. We can't talk of marriage just yet."

"But if I love you and you love me . . ."

"Darling, you're so impetuous! But we must be prudent. We must look at this thing from all angles—go carefully. There's my father . . ."

She broke off. But the expression in her voice was eloquent and had the desired effect of bringing Pat down from the pinnacle of rapture on which he had poised himself.

He lit a cigarette and smoked hard for an instant, his brows contracted. Of course, Sonia was right. He was a crazy fool to let his emotions run away with him like this. He could scarcely expect to propose marriage to Sonia and be accepted on the spot. There was her father to be reckoned with. And Sonia's position *and* his own.

"You do understand, don't you, darling?" came Sonia's soft voice. "It won't do to make our feelings for each other too public, at least not during this trip. You can see how awkward it would be. You've taken Woodham's place, and Daddy would be furious. He might throw up the whole trip and go straight back to London. Then instead of having a lovely few weeks together, there'd be rows and scenes. Oh, I don't want that. I don't want to spoil this holiday. If we're sensible and careful it can be so wonderful for us."

Pat reflected upon this. He had to admit that Sonia was justified in what she said. Obviously, the old man would be outraged at the thought that he, a mere salesman in the firm, acting as chauffeur, should have made love to his daughter. On the other hand, Pat was so much in love that he wanted to proclaim his passion for Sonia to the whole world. He was prepared to face even John Royale and say: "I adore her . . . I want to do something worthy . . . something to deserve her. . . ."

Fine, brave rhapsodies! But coming down to hard, cold facts, what *could* he do? How could he ever be in a position to marry Sonia? How could he expect her to lead the life of a poor man's wife? Or how could he stamp out all that was proud and independent in himself and take on a rich wife . . . even providing that John Royale chose to sanction the match?

"Don't look so worried, darling," said Sonia. "Things will work out, I dare say. Let's just be happy for the next few weeks and keep our love a secret, shall we?"

He threw away his cigarette and took her in his arms again.

"Anything that you say, but I want to do what's right. I don't want to be underhand about this love. . . . I should hate that. . . ."

She bit her lip. He was so very intense and sincere and she would really rather have kept this affair on a lighter basis. Pat Connel was rather a dangerous young man to trifle with. She was well aware of that. She shivered to think what he would say if he knew about Maurice. . . .

"I don't want anything underhand either," she tried to soothe him. "But obviously it will be disastrous if we give ourselves away at the beginning of this journey. We must keep it a secret until we get back to England, mustn't we?"

"Yes, I suppose so," he said reluctantly.

She sighed with relief.

"And then we'll talk about the future."

"There *will* be a future for us, Sonia, won't there? You do really care for me enough to contemplate some sort of life with me?"

Sonia tried to shut out the thought of Maurice . . . and Paris. She murmured:

"Of course. And meanwhile we'll just be frightfully happy and have a marvellous time. There'll be lots of moments when we can be together . . . steal away alone for an hour or two. . . . Daddy will never guess in a thousand years, and my Cousin Jane . . ." Sonia shrugged her shoulders. "We must just be careful of her."

"She's an awfully good sort, is little Jane Daunt," said Pat. "Even if she found out, she'd give us her blessing, don't you think so?"

Sonia gulped. There was an ironic humour in the idea of Jane giving them a blessing . . . Jane of all people in the world.

"M'm. We must go back now," she whispered.

"Tell me once more that you love me and that there's some hope for me . . . one day. . . ."

With his arms about her and his kisses on her lips, Sonia weakened and gave him a dozen promises that she could never keep, a dozen hopes which she knew would never be fulfilled.

Pat drove her back to the hotel feeling a god, a giant, deliriously in love, even ready to go against his better judgement and remain Sonia's lover in secret—because for this journey she wished it to be so.

CHAPTER SIX

JANE DAUNT sat on the edge of her bed transcribing shorthand notes into longhand, which she liked to do while the dictation was still fresh in her memory.

With the shaded lamp by the bedside throwing a soft amber light upon the slight figure in the green silky wrapper, Jane looked more like a child intent upon a puzzle than John Royale's staid young secretary at work. For now the smooth brown hair, usually rolled so neatly at the nape of her neck, was loose and flowed softly almost to her shoulders, making a lovely frame for the pale oval of her face. She looked beautiful. But she looked tired and she felt it, too. She had been writing at her uncle's dictation most of the evening. Now it was ten o'clock, and after the long drive she felt an irresistible desire for sleep.

Where was Sonia? That was what troubled Jane. Her cousin had the room adjoining this one. The communicating door was ajar. Jane could see that Sonia's room was in darkness and knew that she had not come back. Her father thought she had gone to bed. Jane was quite sure that she had slipped out to meet somebody. And that somebody could be no other than Pat Connel.

A deep resentment burned in Jane's breast. It was a resentment that sprang not only from her intimate knowledge of Sonia's affairs, but her secret love for Pat, himself.

He was unattainable. She knew that, and he was madly in love with Sonia. And she, Jane, was sore and angry with him for having come out here like this. He was only making a fool of himself. There could be nothing but catastrophe at the end of it. Yet she could not stop loving him nor wishing with all her heart that she could avert disaster for him.

As for Sonia, no words could describe the sheer anger which Jane felt against her cousin to-night. Why must anybody so lovely be so heartless? Why couldn't she have learnt her lesson in Paris two years ago? And why must she fasten upon Pat Connel, a penniless young man who could never be anything to her, just to gratify her own insatiable vanity?

There could be only one excuse for her, and that was her upbringing. She had lost her mother at a young and impressionable age when she had most needed the guidance and good influence of that mother. And John Royale had spoilt her disgracefully. It was just that . . . she was spoilt . . . and she wanted her own way and cared little, or perhaps thought little, of how much she hurt others in attaining her own desires.

Jane found the thought of Pat and Sonia meeting somewhere out there in the spring starlight interfering badly with her work. She could no longer concentrate on her uncle's descriptions of the French countryside. She shut her notebook with an exasperated gesture and looked at her wristwatch. A quarter past ten. Where *was* that foolish girl?

Suddenly there came the sound of a door opening and shutting and a light flashed on. Jane swung round, went quickly to the communicating door and opened it wide. Sonia stood there, taking off her fur coat. Sonia with fair curls dishevelled, eyes shining, cheeks a richer pink than usual. When she saw Jane she smiled. But Jane met that smile with stern gravity.

"Where on earth have you been, Sonia?"

"Having a little fresh air, darling."

"But you've been gone hours."

"About an hour and a half to be exact, my love."

Jane's lips curved into a humourless smile.

"And I suppose you've been taking a brisk walk in those—"

She pointed to Sonia's high-heeled satin shoes, which showed no signs of stain or dust.

Sonia's smile vanished. She began to take off her dress, yawning.

"Oh, my dear Jane, for heaven's sake don't constitute yourself my keeper. You never have been, and I don't see why you ever should be."

Jane coloured and came forward, nearer her cousin.

"I may not be your keeper, but I'm the best friend you've got, Sonia, and you know it."

Sonia sat down, slender and exquisite in cami-knickers of rich ivory satin and creamy lace. She unbuckled her shoes, still yawning. She was in too good a humour to be really annoyed with Jane. Poor dear Jane must deliver her little lecture and feel better, that was all!

"You're always a dear to me, Janie. But don't interfere with me too much, darling. I don't like it."

"And I suppose," said Jane, with a direct look at her, "you didn't like interference from me when I helped you out of that mess with Maurice?"

"Why bring that up?"

46

"Because, you foolish girl, I know exactly where you've been to-night, and I'm not going to bed until I tell you what I think of you."

"And where *have* I been?" Sonia's grey-green eyes shot a defiant look at her.

"Out with Pat Connel."

For an instant Sonia was tempted to break into angry retort, to say: "And why shouldn't I . . .?" And to taunt Jane with the fact that she was fonder of that young man than she ought to be. But Sonia desisted. She realised that it would be folly to attack Jane in such a manner. Unfortunately Jane had every right to try to stop her from indulging in an affair with Pat, for Jane alone knew about Maurice. On the other hand, Sonia imagined herself thoroughly in love with Pat—for the moment. She was not prepared to give anything up for his sake, but she was prepared to have a very wonderful holiday with him. And the only way to ensure it was to throw dust in Jane's eyes. So she lied coolly and deliberately. Sitting back in her chair, she smiled and shook her head at Jane.

"My dear old thing, you're perfectly right. But you've jumped to wrong conclusions. I went out into the grounds of the hotel and found Connel strolling about taking the air like I was. Naturally, we talked. As I told you this morning, I think he's a very attractive young man. But I did not have an assignation with him. I am *not* altogether forgetting my position — or his."

"You know quite well that he isn't like Woodham."

"On the other hand, he has put himself in Woodham's place and must be treated as such. As a matter of fact, he was inclined to be a little familiar, and that annoyed me, so I ordered him to get out the car and drive me through the town to see the sights. I think he was furious, but he had to do it, and here I am!"

Jane thought:

"My poor old Pat . . . how he must have hated being treated like that! But it's his own fault. . . ."

"I can see, darling," went on Sonia, "that you've taken it for granted that I'm out for a flirtation with Pat Connel. But I'm not. So stop worrying about either of us."

"Right," said Jane. "If that's really how you feel, I'm glad. I want you to leave him alone."

Sonia dabbed her face with cream.

"Why are *you* so interested in him, darling?" she asked casually.

But Jane was not giving herself away. She answered as casually:

"We're just good friends and always have been since he worked for the firm. I know how attractive you are, Sonia, and how much he admires you. I don't think it would be fair of you to fool round with him."

With slim finger-tips Sonia worked the cream into her cheeks. Cheeks that were still stinging from the passionate kisses of her lover. And she was thinking:

"I don't want to fool round . . . I want Pat to love me . . . I want to love him . . . and we're not going to be stopped by Jane or anybody else."

Aloud she said:

"You needn't worry, Janie. I'm not going to hurt your Irishman. Let's not harp on the subject, because it's rather boring. I'm enjoying this tour, aren't you?"

Jane came behind her and dropped a kiss on the fair head.

"Very much. But I'm tired. You look simply glowing. I don't know how you manage it. Good night, dear. I'm off to sleep."

For an instant Sonia was tempted to turn round and pour the whole of her heart out to her cousin. She was really very devoted to Jane. Jane had been such a stand-by, such a comfort, such a tower of strength all through that awful Paris episode. And Sonia had her good instincts. She was more thoughtless than unkind. Most of her faults sprang from sheer egotism and vanity. She adored admiration and excitement. She needed emotionalism. And she did not see why she should be made to go on paying for ever for her folly with Maurice. Besides which, Pat Connel was desperately in love with her. She wasn't hurting him. She was being very kind and responsive. She was going to make him happy.

Her limpid eyes filled with sudden tears. They were tears of self-pity. She was awfully sorry for herself because of Maurice. She wished she was free to return Pat's love . . . had a right to accept him or any other man as a lover.

Jane saw the flash of tears and was immediately tender and solicitous. She put an arm round her cousin.

"What is it, honey?"

Sonia hid her eyes against Jane's shoulder.

"Nothing . . . but I was just thinking . . . how cruel life has been. If only there wasn't Maurice. . . ."

"Poor darling. I know. I wish there was some way out."

"But there isn't," said Sonia in a muffled voice, "and so I must go on being good. Somehow, to-night, I've been thinking about Francis."

"Francis Glyde? But why?"

"Well, you know how much he's in love with me—wants to marry me. I'm afraid I was rather encouraging to him. Now I'm away from England I must write him a little note and tell him that it's hopeless."

Jane nodded. So it was of Francis Glyde that Sonia had been thinking . . . and of those shackles which were preventing her from accepting any offers of marriage . . . poor little Sonia! Jane stayed a while comforting her, talking to her. The memory of Pat Connel was forgotten. Jane was thrown completely off the scent and went to bed satisfied.

But after Jane had gone, Sonia wept again in secret. And the tears were not for Francis Glyde, but for Pat. She was genuinely miserable because she suddenly realised that the love which Pat was offering her differed from any of the other loves in her life. It was something big and enthralling, which she wanted badly and which she dared not take. And that did not suit Sonia Royale, who had had practically everything in the world that she wanted until now.

Jane, thinking things over in her own room, felt overwhelming relief, because Sonia had no real interest in Pat.

Perhaps the journey to Morocco would be a success after all. Not that her own position, so far as Pat was concerned, could alter in any way. But she could put up with that so long as she knew that he would not have his heart broken or his life ruined by Sonia.

Long before either her uncle or her cousin were up, Jane was dressed and downstairs and standing on the front steps of the hotel. The sky was clear and blue and the April morning fresh and exhilarating.

While she stood there, feeling suddenly hungry for her breakfast, she saw the Victor come into view round the corner of the garage. She watched it draw up at the side of the steps. Pat, at the wheel, looking fresh and attractive in his green uniform, caught sight of Jane and saluted her. She went down the steps and greeted him.

"Good morning, Pat."

"Good morning, miss."

"Now, Pat, drop that."

He grinned at her like a boy.

"Top of the morning to you, then, mavourneen."

"And hardly *that*."

"Then, hullo to you, Jane."

"That's better." She smiled, and taking a cigarette-case from the pocket of her short suède coat which she wore over a polo jersey, she offered it to him. "Have one?"

"And what will the head porter of the Hôtel de Ville think if he sees one of the mademoiselles offering a cigarette in that familiar fashion to the chauffeur?"

Nevertheless, he took one and thanked her.

"You're a silly idiot to have come in Woodham's place," Jane remarked in her blunt fashion.

"But I'm enjoying it thoroughly."

"You look as though you are."

"I am," he smiled gaily. "It's much more amusing than trying to sell cars to people who haven't any money."

"Well, so long as it amuses you . . ." She shrugged her shoulders.

"Are you still cross with me for coming?"

"I still think it was a foolish thing for you to do."

"Ah, but you don't know how sensible it really was!"

She looked at him steadily. She was not quite sure why he was in such excellent spirits. Just for an instant she had a faint, horrid little suspicion that what Sonia had told her last night was not strictly true. Had she really snubbed Pat and been indifferent to him? If so, why wasn't he sunk in gloom, instead of sitting on top of the world? Still, Pat was like that . . . always trying to get on top of the world, if not actually achieving it.

"Aren't you enjoying the trip?" he asked her.

"I think so."

"It's sure to be marvellous driving through France this time of the year, and when we get to Spain it'll be hot and sunny, and in Morocco warmer still. By the way, Spain's a most romantic place."

"We've come for the purpose of giving my uncle a holiday rather than for romance," said Jane drily.

Pat looked at the point of his cigarette. He felt suddenly guilty. He would like to have told little Jane Daunt just how filled with wild romance this tour would be . . . for him . . . and for Sonia. But that was impossible. He had agreed that they must keep their love a secret . . . that for all their sakes he must say nothing until Sonia gave the word and the time be propitious for him to announce that they loved each other and that he had asked her to marry him.

The fact that their love needed all this secrecy was a fact to be deplored, but for Pat it could not destroy the essential thrill of it. He looked kindly upon Jane's pale young face and wondered suddenly what lay behind her gravity, her reserve.

"Do you never allow yourself a romantic thought?" he asked her. "Are you always so darned practical and efficient?"

Her brown eyes smouldered, but revealed nothing. And it was not given to him to know that in the very depths of her being Jane Daunt was essentially romantic . . . that her heart was starved for romance . . . that at the mere idea of the warm sunny days and the moonlit nights in Spain and in North Africa, so close to *him*, her whole soul was shaken, yes, shaken—but to no purpose. For this love that she bore him was to no purpose, and therefore must be concealed. She would have died before letting him guess what she felt, so she put up a bluff which he found impenetrable.

"I haven't time for romance," she said. "I'm much too busy, and I should imagine you are too."

"Oh, sure!" he laughed, but there was mockery in those very blue eyes of his. And he, too, was giving away nothing this morning.

Then the voice of John Royale interrupted their conversation.

"Ah! There you are, Jane. And Connel too. He's a bit

early. We haven't had breakfast. But I prefer people to be too early than too late."

Pat Connel slipped back into Woodham's place. He touched his cap.

"Good morning, sir."

"Another half an hour and we'll push off," said John Royale, rubbing his hands. "Have you looked at the map, Connel? Do you know where we shall land next?"

"Yes, sir. We go about one hundred and thirty-nine kilometres to Tours, and then through to Poitiers, and with good luck and the Victor doing its best, we ought to be in Bordeaux to-night."

"Excellent," said Royale, "excellent!"

"Hullo, everybody," said a sweet, high voice.

Jane and the two men looked up. On the balcony of the first floor stood the figure of Sonia, fair as the spring morning in a daffodil-yellow dress of soft wool material, and a small Marina hat of the same colour at the side of her blonde curls.

She waved to them.

"All set for the day's journey?"

"All set, my dear," called back her father.

Jane looked at Pat. And her heart seemed suddenly to miss a beat when she saw the expression on his face. He was staring up at Sonia. In his eyes, so very blue under their thick black lashes, lay a passionate adoration which was horribly revealing to Jane. Equally revealing was the look which Sonia was giving him. Jane, intercepting it, felt the colour burn her cheeks and her heart sink. There was something more than instinct now to make her suspicious. She *knew* that Sonia had lied to her last night, and that there was *something* between those two. Something that was bound to destroy Pat in the end . . . Pat with all his ambitions, his gay courage, his ideals.

Jane turned and walked up the steps into the hotel.

All the radiance of the morning had fled for her. She could only face a tangle of thoughts and ideas and emotions, ask herself what she could do, and know, even while she asked, that the answer was—*"Nothing!"*

CHAPTER SEVEN

IT could not be said that Jane enjoyed the rest of that drive through France. By the time they reached the Spanish border, still less was she enjoying herself.

That look which she had intercepted between Sonia and Pat on the morning of their departure from Chartres was only the beginning of a dozen and one little incidents which strengthened her suspicions that these two were having a secret *affaire*.

Mile after mile through the radiant spring days Sonia would sit beside the driver of the big grey car, always a little closer than was necessary, never failing at intervals to give him the full benefit of her lovely eyes. Always Jane Daunt sat at the back of the car with her uncle, and, when she wasn't taking down notes, was forced to watch Pat, who, in his turn, glanced constantly at Sonia's exquisite profile. Such glances left Jane no room for doubt what lay in his mind. He was madly in love with Sonia.

But what game Sonia was playing, Jane could not guess. Sonia was so reticent nowadays. She lied—quite shamelessly, of course—whenever Jane questioned her.

Jane could hardly accuse her of lying, nor had she any real right to interfere, except that it was almost beyond her endurance to be a silent witness of Pat's downfall. For what else could it mean for him except a downfall? If Sonia was tempting him, playing with him, there must inevitably be a rude awakening for him.

John Royale, engrossed in his literary work, sa[...]
of the little drama which was being performed un[der]
his very eyes. He presumed that the two girls were enjoying themselves, and Connel was a magnificent driver,
more useful than Woodham could ever have been, so he
was content.

They stayed a couple of days in Biarritz, where Mr.
Royale abandoned his work for a game of golf on those
famous and lovely links.

That was a particularly trying morning for Jane. Her
uncle insisted upon taking her with him.

"You don't play golf, but you can be my caddy, and
the exercise will do you good after all the driving and
typing," he told her.

He wanted Sonia to go, too. But Sonia managed to have
a "headache" and announced that she must lie down and
rest. Later, she said, she would get Connel to drive her
along the sea-front to see the sights of the gay, fashionable
watering-place.

Jane knew what that meant! Sonia was planning a few
hours alone with Pat. What could come of it, Jane dared
not think. With a heavy heart she went off to the golf
links with her uncle and left the other two behind.

Sonia spent that fresh sparkling morning in exactly
the manner which Jane predicted. The moment her father
and cousin were safely stowed away on the golf course and
Pat had returned with the car, Sonia joined him and went
out. There was no lying abed for her. In one of her most
attractive outfits — grey flannel suit, white jersey, and spot-
ted scarf—looking as radiant as a June rose, Sonia
allowed Pat to drive her out of the town and a little way
into the country, where they could talk.

The moment they were in a secluded spot, Pat, his handsome face quite pale with emotion, took the lovely figure
in his arms and kissed her passionately on lips and throat.

sweet . . ."

...ously as she leaned against him.

...s."

...Do you know, I haven't kissed you once ...Bordeaux."

...that seems a long time ago."

...s an eternity between each time that I kiss you," she smiled.

"What a born lover you are."

"And you were born to be loved because you're so beautiful."

He kissed her again. Then, when the first ecstatic moments were fled, he drew away from her and grew sane again and suddenly grave.

"You know I don't like it, Sonia. All this secrecy worries me."

"Darling, aren't you getting used to it?"

"No, I don't think I ever shall. It doesn't suit my temperament. I'd far rather go straight to your father to-night, and tell him that I want to marry you—infernal, colossal impudence though it might seem."

Sonia's slim figure tautened.

"You can't do that. You mustn't."

"Oh, I know all the arguments," he said, frowning, "and I dare say it would break up everything; but I don't like going behind his back in this way."

"Neither do I, darling. But it would be mad to let conscience worry us too much and spoil our whole trip."

Her slim white hand stole up and caressed the black handsome head which attracted her so vitally. She tried to woo him from his feelings of guilt. But Pat was persistent this morning. It seemed that he worried much more about the situation than she did, although, she told herself, she had more cause to worry than he. For didn't she know that while that wretched Maurice existed, there could be no way out for her and for Pat.

"Are you sure your cousin Jane doesn't guess about us?" he asked her.

Sonia lit a cigarette and smoked it as she leaned back in the circle of his arm.

"I dare say—but what does it matter?"

With a half-humorous smile, he looked down at her perfect profile.

"Do you know, darling, I believe women are more unscrupulous than men. You don't worry that beautiful head of yours very much about this intrigue. But I do. Take Jane, for instance. She's always been a good friend to me. Sometimes she looks at me very reproachfully, as though she knows, and it makes me feel a bit of a cad. I suppose I *am* a cad, making love to my Chief's daughter behind his back."

"Not at all, since the Chief's daughter wishes you to do so and has asked you to say nothing about it," murmured Sonia. "And as for Jane, we really can't live our lives to please *her*."

"I suppose nothing matters so long as you really love me and will marry me one day and let me win the world for you," he said, intoxicated by the touch of her hand and the nearness of her.

Because a faint flush stole into her cheeks and a faint expression of dismay came into her eyes, she hid her face against his shoulder and embraced him mutely. Wherefore he took her silence to mean assent.

When they returned to the hotel after those few stolen hours, Pat was completely won over again, ready to do anything that Sonia commanded of him.

But Sonia in her queer way was not quite so pleased with life to-day. Once she was alone, she was pursued by her thoughts and memories. It was the memory of

Maurice, her husband with whom she had lived for only a few days, which haunted her most persistently. Where was he now? How much longer would he insist on extorting money for her silence? And why, why couldn't she secure a divorce as secretly and effectively as she had effected that mad marriage?

Much as her father loved her, she knew that this thing, were it to come to his knowledge, would shock him horribly. He was the straightest man in the world, and he detested any kind of deception or underhand dealing. Sonia was beginning to be afraid ... afraid, too, of Jane. Jane knew so much, and Jane was obviously attracted by Pat. Sonia could not but be aware that it was a very dangerous game which she was playing.

She had a little present waiting for Jane when she came back from the golf course. In a perverted fashion it salved her conscience a bit to be extra nice to Jane.

"Connel drove me into the town, and I found this for you, darling," she told her cousin languidly. She was lying on her bed, still keeping up the pretence of the headache.

Jane, brown and flushed after walking those eighteen holes in the wind and sun of the April morning, looked gravely at Sonia and then at the present—a blue-and-rose cashmere handkerchief-scarf.

"It's Molyneux, darling," murmured Sonia.

"It's lovely," said Jane, "and thanks awfully."

But her shrewd little brain knew perfectly well what this present meant. That mad girl had been out the whole morning with Pat, and this was a silent method of expressing remorse. If only she would *tell her* what she was doing ... what she meant to do about Pat!

Jane could scarcely trust herself to stay in the room and speak to Sonia. Her nerves were jangling. And that was unusual for Jane, who was, as a rule, so cool and poised. She was in a state of nerves for the rest of that day, and it culminated in an unhappy scene that night. She had known that it could only be a question of time before the intrigue between Sonia and Pat was discovered. Sonia was missing after dinner, and Jane was expected to do some work. But she was unable to put her mind to it. She was so worried about those two. And not only worried, but conscious of an entirely feminine jealousy. Why must Sonia, who could never marry any man till she was rid of Maurice, take the one man whom she, Jane, had ever loved? Why must Pat, who was so dear to her, have eyes and ears only for Sonia? It wasn't fair!

There was bitterness in Jane's heart as she excused herself from her uncle and walked out into the moonlit grounds of the big hotel in search of Sonia.

The luxuriant palms spread dark spiky shadows against the luminous sky and the air was rich and sweet with the scent of mimosa. Jane, with a short fur coat over her evening dress, wandered here and there, conscious in a queer, fatalistic fashion that she was going to find Sonia and Pat together. She did not want to find them . . . all that was most fastidious and proud in her shrank from it . . . but she had to go on, propelled by something stronger than herself.

She came upon them, at length, sitting in an arbour which looked upon a small Italian garden with stone-paved pathways and white statues among the flowers. She felt her heart flick and hurt horribly as she saw. She stood stock-still.

Pat, wearing a grey suit instead of the chauffeur's uniform, was standing there, with Sonia in his arms. Sonia's white fur wrap barely concealed a glittering evening dress which was made of some exquisite spun-gloss material. The moonlight seemed to radiate a million lights from it. And only too plainly Jane saw those two faces, both so beautiful in their own way, blurred into one during that passionate embrace.

Then Pat caught sight of the watching figure, and with an exclamation he released Sonia.

"God, there's Cousin Jane!" he said under his breath.

Sonia swung round. For a moment she was speechless with dismay. How in heaven's name had Jane found them here? Was it by mistake, or had she deliberately followed? For an instant anger surged through Sonia. She was not going to be spied upon, no matter whether Maurice existed or not . . . she was going to tell Jane so. She was about to speak, but Jane turned and ran away . . . ran as though the sight of the lovers was unbearable to her.

Pat drew a hand across his forehead.

"That's torn it," he said.

"Damn," said Sonia under her breath.

"I'm afraid there's no doubt in her mind about us now. Sonia, I was a crazy fool to let you meet me like this. I felt that we were taking an awful risk. And yet I had to see you. . . . I wanted to . . ."

She flung herself back into his arms.

"Don't worry. I'll deal with Jane."

"What will you say?"

"Oh, something . . ."

"But you won't be able to deny it. . . ."

"No, I won't try, but I'll just tell Jane to mind her own business."

Pat released her.

"I told you this morning that I didn't like it, darling. It's all so secretive and . . ."

She stopped him with a fragrant hand against his lips.

"We've had that all out. You know why we must keep silence. It's for your sake as well as mine. I'll deal with Jane. Don't worry."

"Very well," he said wretchedly.

But the glamour of the evening had fled for Pat. He felt small and humiliated. He disliked having been seen by Jane Daunt like that. She must think him an awful bounder. She wasn't the kind of girl to countenance deceit, and he wouldn't blame her for despising him. But he must see her to-morrow and tell her frankly that he wanted to marry Sonia, and he was going to live and work with that one aim and object in his mind.

Surely she would admit that love gave him a certain right . . . real love such as this. She would forgive him when she knew that it wasn't just a passing passion . . . an ugly hole-and-corner temporary affair.

The lovers lingered for only another swift embrace, and then Sonia ran back to the hotel.

She went straight to Jane's bedroom and found the door locked.

"Jane," she called, "let me in."

Jane very reluctantly opened that door. Her face was pale and stern. Sonia avoided her gaze, but went straight to the point.

"I suppose you're furious with me. But you shouldn't have come spying. Then you wouldn't have known."

"I prefer to know," said Jane.

But even as she said the words, she wondered if that was true. She felt that she would be haunted night and day by the picture of those two figures merged into one, like a graceful statue of love out there in the Italian garden. Fine lovers, both of them. But Sonia was not for Pat, and Pat might have been *hers* if Sonia, with her cruel egotism and lack of regard for another's pain, hadn't drawn him into her own white arms.

"Well," said Sonia defiantly, "what about it?"

CHAPTER EIGHT

THE long hateful scene was over. Sonia had gone and Jane was alone again.

She felt that as long as she lived she never wanted to see Biarritz again. She felt that it was a place in which she had been betrayed. Sonia was a traitor to her word, and Pat Connel to his own intelligence. Sonia was selfish and cruel. But Pat was crazy, blinded by this infatuation, enslaved by a woman's beauty and seductiveness. He must *know* that he could not play such a game with his Chief's daughter and get away with it. Even though he was serious—and Jane was sure that was so—it was all incredibly foolish of him. He could never hope to marry Sonia. It would have been difficult even if she had been free, but as things were it was impossible.

For two solid hours Jane had argued and protested with her cousin, used every ounce of strength that she possessed to try to make Sonia see that she could not, must not, let this affair continue. For two hours she had pleaded, begging Sonia to let Pat alone, if only for his sake.

And for two hours Sonia had listened and remained stubborn. From defiance she had changed to pathos. She had assured Jane that she was really in love with Pat Connel and wanted a little happiness in her life. And when Jane had pointed out that it was a gross injustice to Pat to take her happiness at the expense of his, Sonia had changed again. What sympathy she might have commanded she lost by becoming spiteful. She had ended by telling Jane that the main trouble with her was that she was *jealous*.

"You want him yourself!" she had said. "You're angry because I've got him—that's all."

It was those words which lingered to hurt Jane cruelly long after Sonia's exit from the room. It was a shaft that hit near the truth and yet was not quite true. She could not deny that she loved Pat Connel. But she did not deplore this affair because she, personally, wanted him. She would have tried to be glad about the affair had it been for his happiness. Or if Sonia had been honest, told him about Maurice, and he had still wanted to be her lover, she, Jane, might have deplored the folly of it; but she could have washed her hands of the business then and let them get on with it. But these circumstances were so different. Sonia was afraid to tell the truth, and Pat was being exalted crazily to a height from which he must inevitably crash. It was that thought which hit Jane so hard. She wanted so passionately to save him.

She could do nothing about it. Her hands were hopelessly tied. The last thing Sonia had done to-night was to remind her that she had taken a vow two years ago never to reveal the fact of her marriage to anybody on earth. Jane knew that she must keep silence; just stand by and see this affair continue and let Pat be dragged to his ruin.

Jane could understand Pat's attitude. He was a volatile, impressionable young Irishman with a terrific amount of vitality and enthusiasm for life, and Sonia was as beautiful as a poet's dream and kind to him . . . sweet and kind. Nobody knew better than Jane how adorable Sonia could be when she chose.

But what would he feel when he learned the truth, which he must eventually do? Sonia might imagine that he would be content to carry on with this intrigue, but Jane knew that such was not the case. He was straight, and he would want to put things on a straight and proper footing. Then Sonia would either have to tell him the facts about Maurice—or send him away.

Jane slept badly that night. She woke with a wretched little feeling that everything was spoilt now. There could be no further enjoyment for her during this tour. It would be nothing but an agony for her to sit in the background and watch Pat's reckless pursuit of Sonia.

It rained that day, and so John Royale abandoned his plans for spending another morning on the links, and they moved on from Biarritz through Saint Jean de Luz, and so to Hendaye and the Spanish frontier.

Here Pat Connel made himself very useful with his knowledge of Spain, the language, and people. With great ease he got them through the Spanish customs.

If it hadn't been for her worries, Jane would thoroughly have enjoyed this day which marked their entry into Spain. This was gorgeous country and wonderful weather. Spain was at her loveliest in the spring. White walls, blue skies, the verdant green of barley fields splashed with scarlet poppies, an occasional glimpse of sapphire sea. Picturesque peasants on their little grey donkeys, girls with coloured shawls and flowers. Black-eyed babies, beautiful as Murillo paintings, sprawling in the sunlit doorways of cottages which were half-covered with bright cerise bougainvillæa. An atmosphere which seemed utterly different from any other in the world.

In the afternoon they traversed a sinuous road flanked by woodlands, and so ascended through the violet-blue mountains, which were savage and splendid against the vivid sky. Through San Sebastian and Tolosa and Vittoria, they came at the setting of the sun to Burgos, where they spent the night.

It had been a day of driving which Pat had enjoyed more than anything. Especially those hairpin bends in the ascent of the Puerto de Echegarate. He was a little proud of his fine driving, and well rewarded when Sonia whispered:

"I wouldn't have had Woodham through this for anything. You're *marvellous*!"

Jane heard those words. They made her slightly sick. Resentment burned in her young breast.

"Why can't she leave him alone?" was her inward thought.

Later that evening Jane found the first opportunity since leaving Biarritz to speak alone with Pat.

She had dropped her favourite fountain-pen out of her bag in the back of the car. She went round to the hotel garage to find it. Pat, in his shirt-sleeves and gum-boots, was washing the dust and dirt off the big Victor. A cigarette was stuck on his lower lip, and he was whistling cheerfully. As he saw Jane approach, he took the cigarette from his lips and bowed from the waist.

"*Buenos, Señorita.*"

"That," said Jane, "means 'Hail', or something, I suppose."

'It's an ordinary Spanish greeting."

"Very proud of yourself, aren't you?"

His blue eyes danced at her.

"Very."

She bit her lip. There flashed across her memory that unforgettable vision of Pat as she had seen him in the garden at Biarritz with Sonia in his arms. And somehow Pat's intuition told him what she was thinking. He, too, remembered. He ceased being flippant. A slow red crept up under the tan of his face. He came and stood beside her.

"Jane Daunt, are you thoroughly disgusted with me because of the other night? You look it."

She, too, flushed red and did not meet his gaze. Then before she could restrain herself, she said coldly:

"I came to fetch my fountain-pen. Have you seen it, Connel?"

The flush left his cheeks. He went rather white and immediately clicked his heels together.

"Yes, miss. I have it here."

He drew the pen from his pocket and handed it to her.

Immediately Jane regretted her tone and implication. It was mean of her to remind Pat that he had come as a chauffeur. She said impulsively:

"Oh, Pat, why are you being such a *fool*?"

He looked steadily down at her.

"Now, are we friends . . . or just Miss Daunt and servant?"

"You know we're friends."

"Sure, I thought so until you spoke just now."

"I was angry."

"I know. What you saw the other night upset you. Perhaps you have a right to be upset. You think it mean of me—beastly—to make love to Sonia behind her father's back."

"What do *you* think about it?"

His eyes glowed.

"I can think of nothing but her and the fact that I love her more than anything in the world."

Jane swallowed hard.

"You've always been ambitious, Pat. But isn't this a little *too* optimistic of you?"

"You mean because I'm a salesman without a sou and she's—Miss Royale?"

Jane nodded. She meant so much more than that . . . so much that she could not say.

"I admit that it sounds damned impudent, but she has given me the right to hope. You see, Jane, Sonia loves me as much as I do her."

Jane turned from him. For an instant she felt an absurd inclination to burst into tears. It was so hopeless and so pathetic. She was so terribly in love with him. It hurt like mad to hear him talk this way about another woman . . . and that woman one who could never be anything more to him than she was now.

"You might as well know about it," continued Pat. "Sonia won't mind me telling you. . . . I expect she's told you herself that we love each other. You can't doubt it after seeing us at Biarritz."

"Pat, Pat," said Jane in a low voice, "where can it all lead to?"

His gay, insouciant smile flashed out.

"The altar, I hope."

"You want to . . . marry her?"

"That is my one ambition . . . or one of my many, shall I say? Sonia has asked me to keep all this secret from her father until we return to England because she is afraid that it might spoil the whole tour."

"Uncle John would never consent."

"Does money make all that difference, Jane? Or is it just that I'm not good enough for her?"

She swung round then, cheeks flaming.

"Of course you're good enough. . . . Why shouldn't you be? But it's all so difficult . . ."

"Don't fash yourself, little Jane Daunt," said Pat in his peculiarly tender Irish voice. "Don't worry. I can manage my own affairs, and I believe implicitly in Sonia. She has her reasons for not wanting me to be honest about my love for her for the moment."

"Yes," said Jane under her breath, "she has her reasons. . . ."

"I feel rotten about deceiving the old man, but it *would* spoil his holiday if I told him, wouldn't it?"

67

He caught Jane's eye and smiled whimsically. She tried to smile back.

"Undoubtedly."

"Then forgive me and don't be too hard on either of us. Just wish us luck."

She found it impossible to utter the words that he wanted to hear. He added:

"If I ever have the great good luck to make Sonia my wife, you and I will be sort of related, eh, mavourneen?"

She could bear no more. The desire to weep became too strong for her. She took the pen and turned and ran out of the garage.

For a moment she stood outside the hotel, trying to recover her composure before she joined her uncle and tackled her transcription.

What a lovely night, she thought! There was something about Spain which appealed vastly to Jane. She loved all that was uncivilised about it. She liked to see the women in their shawls with flowers behind their ears strolling with their lovers through the starry darkness. She liked to hear the faint sound of a tango rhythm, the click of a castanet, and the sweet tenor voice of some young singer chanting an old Spanish air with peculiar passion and melancholy.

She had never felt so sad in her life. Nothing seemed worth while. The man she loved was in love with somebody else, and he was going to be badly hurt at the end of it all.

Even while she stood there, sorrowfully contemplating the night, she saw a shadowy figure in white emerge from the hotel, hurry round the corner, and vanish. It was Sonia. Sonia stealing out to bid good night to her lover.

Jane's all too vivid imagination pictured the meeting between the two. Pat's gay face would become eager and passionate. He would open his arms and take Sonia into a close embrace. . . .

A little sob rose in Jane's throat. She turned and ran quickly into the hotel.

CHAPTER NINE

AND so to Madrid!

The brilliant laughing capital of Spain was a little uneasy. The shadow of recent revolution lurked in the corners and unrest brooded over the people. But the place was still vivid enough and full of a careless charm which appealed in particular to Jane. Madrid was the very heart of the most romantic country in the world. In a way, it intensified her loneliness, for she had to stand by knowing that Pat and Sonia were absorbed in each other, ever wondering what the end would be.

The first night in Madrid marked a disaster. Jane, following much the same routine as usual, dined with her uncle and cousin. And after coffee had been served, she retreated with Mr. Royale to a quiet part of the lounge to take down notes of the day.

Sonia made the mistake of taking it for granted that these two would be nicely engrossed with work for the next hour or so and it never entered her head that her father would take it into his to go out again to-night.

But Mr. Royale, thoroughly interested in the Spanish capital, found himself bored with dictation, and after a brief spell of it, decided to put on his hat and go out for a walk.

If he wanted local colour he could get it strolling past the brightly lit cafés and shops. It was warm enough on this starry, windless night for Spanish folk to sit out under the striped awnings, sip their wine, smoke their cigarettes, and exchange endless philosophies and jests while the rest of their country fermented about their ears.

Mr. Royale suggested that Jane should put on a coat and accompany him, and she, feeling restless, was only too glad to do so.

She ran upstairs to her room to fetch the coat. So far as she knew Sonia had gone to bed, having pleaded a headache. She put her head inside Sonia's room to bid her good night and was surprised to find the room empty. The bed was turned down and a flowered chiffon night-gown spread in readiness, but no Sonia.

Jane went along to both the bathrooms on that floor. They were dark and empty. So Sonia was not having a bath. Therefore Sonia had not come upstairs at all although, after dinner, she had announced her intention of going straight to bed.

Now what was the foolish girl doing, Jane asked herself with set lips? She would certainly get herself entangled if she wasn't careful. However, there was no time for Jane to search farther for her cousin. Uncle John was waiting. Jane joined him and they went out together into the radiant night.

Sonia, meanwhile, walked arm-in-arm with her lover through the Puerta del Sol, the largest of the plazas in Madrid and through the Calle de Alcala toward the Buen Retrio park.

They walked gaily, happily like hundreds of other lovers who strolled through the Spanish streets, some of which were bordered with feathery acacias, silvered by moonlight, and great palms splaying fantastically against the luminous sky.

"You only want a shawl and I could address you as Señorita," said Pat. "Only you're a lot more attractive than any of these Spanish women."

"Some of them are supposed to be raving beauties."

"I can only see *you*," he said.

She pressed his arm to her side with a little murmur of appreciation. She had not yet grown tired of her lover's adulation. It was sweet food for her vanity.

"Aren't we quite mad to be doing this?" he asked her. "Are you quite sure you won't be missed?"

"No. I said good night to Daddy and left him working with Jane. He won't disturb me, and if Jane comes up and looks for me and doesn't find me there—well, she can think what she likes. I don't care."

Pat thought a moment of Jane Daunt's frank questioning eyes and that expression of disapproval which he had seen once or twice lately on her small face.

"Cousin Jane isn't at all pleased about us, is she?" he said.

Sonia made no reply, beyond a shrug of the shoulders. She knew so much better than Pat why Jane wasn't pleased. Jane had every right to be angry and disapproving, but Sonia could scarcely explain *that* to Pat!

They found a café, sat down at a little round marble-topped table, drank strong black coffee in tall glasses and watched the world go by.

It intrigued Sonia to hear Pat talking fluent Spanish to the waiters. He seemed to have forgotten none of the language which he had learnt in his youth. And it intrigued Pat to see the many devouring glances which his companion received from the Spaniards who passed her by.

"You're much too lovely to be safe," he told her, smiling. "I doubt if any of these fellows have seen anything look quite as angelic as you do in their lives before."

For a moment Sonia's conscience stabbed her, for tiny though it was, that conscience existed. She looked at him wistfully.

"I'm not really angelic, Pat."

"You are, my sweet."

"Do you really think I'm—so perfect?"

"Definitely. For how many girls are there in the world who are as good as they're beautiful?"

Sonia bit her lip.

"How do you know I'm so good, Pat?"

"I feel you are, darling."

"Don't you imagine I've ever had a love affair before?"

"I've never allowed myself to imagine anything about it. It's perfectly obvious that a girl who looks like you do and has had all the chances you've had, must also have had dozens of admirers."

"But you don't think I've ever admired anybody in my turn?"

"You're being very serious all of a sudden, Beautiful."

"I want to be," she persisted, urged by something unusually serious within herself. "I want to know if you think I've ever been in love before."

"I think that I'd rather not know. I might feel jealous," he said. "and in any case, whatever affair you've had is over, and you're going to marry me. That's all that matters."

Sonia felt her throat go dry. She dived in her bag for a little gold cigarette-case and put a cigarette between her lips. Pat leaned forward to light it for her and for an instant she saw the burning sincerity in those very blue eyes of his. It seemed to go straight to her heart. There arose in her the most genuine feeling of remorse which she had ever known . . . remorse that she should be deceiving a man who believed in her so implicitly . . . infinite regret that there had ever been a Maurice in her life.

"Pat," she said in a husky voice, "what would you do if I didn't mean to marry you and was just . . . having an affair?"

For an instant he looked startled, then sat back and laughed.

"Don't let's play about with suppositions like that. They're too unpleasant. I think it would just kill me, that's all. I've always been ambitious, but it's more than an ordinary ambition, my desire to make good some way and have you for my wife."

Sonia felt suddenly that she could not sit here and talk any more. All that was best in her seemed to be well to the surface to-night. She was afraid that she might break down and confess and tell Pat that she was already married. And that would be madness . . . that would take him right away from her. He would never understand. She was not brave enough to take the risk and perhaps lose what seemed at the moment so worth retaining . . . his love and his belief in her.

"Let's go back to the hotel," she said abruptly.

He looked at her with some consternation.

"Is there anything wrong, my darling?"

"No, nothing. I'm just tired."

They reached the hotel and stood a moment on the wide steps which led up to a kind of covered terrace where meals were served in the summer. Just for a moment Sonia cast discretion to the winds and flung herself into her lover's arms. She felt suddenly unutterably depressed. She had set out on this assignation in the highest of spirits. Now they had sunk to zero. She curved an arm about Pat's neck and drew his lips down to hers.

"Oh Pat, darling, I hate saying good night and goodbye."

He kissed the warm velvet mouth raised to his, his senses reeling. She had never seemed so close to him, so much in love.

At last she let him go, bade him a last good night and started to walk up the steps. He stood watching the slim figure in the fur coat, and was struck suddenly by something almost tragic in the droop of her head. She was unhappy, his adored love! The thought went through his heart like a knife. Incautiously he sprang up those steps after her and caught her in his arms.

"Darling . . . darling . . . wait . . . don't go. . . ."

And that was the precise moment in which John Royale and Jane chose to return to the hotel from their promenade.

Jane saw . . . and felt the colour scorch her cheeks, then drain away. Those two . . . ye gods, what utter folly . . . right in the front entrance! Mr. Royale saw and stood rooted to the ground.

"Good God!" he said.

His exclamation was loud enough to reach Pat, who released Sonia and swung round as though he had been shot.

"Oh, lord," he said under his breath. "That's done it!"

John Royale marched up the steps. He had but a confused impression of what he had seen. He just took it for granted that his chauffeur or salesman, or whatever he liked to call himself, was forcing his attentions upon Sonia. There was the poor child, struggling with him! They had only just come in time.

"Connel, what the devil does this mean?" he demanded, white with rage.

Pat straightened. The Irish fighting blood in him rose. If this was to be a battle he would plunge into it without fear. He would fight for Sonia, and she was worth fighting for. But her thoughts were not so brave. All her love and desire for Pat was submerged in fear . . . the fear of discovery.

Pat said:

"Look here, sir, I think I'd better tell you . . ."

"Wait!" interrupted Sonia breathlessly.

"Sonia, my darling girl," came from Mr. Royale, and put an arm about her. "What a fright this must have given you. I'm appalled . . . appalled to think that this young man should have taken such a liberty."

She looked at her father speechlessly. She realised that he had taken it for granted that Pat's advances were unwelcome. She also knew that Pat was on the verge of making a full confession about their love for each other. He was always wanting to do the straight and honourable thing. But it could not be allowed to happen. First of all, her father would never consent to their union, but even if he did she, herself, could never consent because of Maurice. Then that whole wretched story would be revealed.

"How dared you, Connel!" thundered Mr. Royale.

Pat looked straight at him, then turned his head slowly and looked at Sonia. Was she going to say anything? She was. She said:

"It wasn't altogether Connel's fault."

John Royale stared.

"What do you mean? Are you suggesting that you encouraged such behaviour?"

Jane, standing in the background, waited breathlessly for Sonia's next words. She, knowing so much, wondered whether her cousin would have the courage to speak the truth. But Sonia was speaking half-truths—anxious not to let all the blame fall upon Pat, and at the same time not to incriminate herself too far.

"I—I wanted a little fresh air and I came out and I—ran into Connel," she stammered. "We were talking, and I . . ."

"And he took advantage and tried to kiss you. I tell you I'm appalled!" said Mr. Royale, his temper well roused.

"Now, Daddy, don't jump to hasty conclusions," began Sonia, her lips trembling. "I—"

"You're just trying to excuse the fellow, because you're soft-hearted," broke in her father. "No, Sonia, I'm not going to have it." He turned on Pat, "I'll not hear any excuses, young man. You've gone too far. What you want is a good hiding and if I had a whip I'd give it to you. You can consider yourself dismissed."

Pat went white. For the moment he was too dumb-founded to reply. Sonia was near to fainting. She made another desperate attempt to calm her father down, but Mr. Royale in a temper was never a man to be argued or reasoned with. He had taken it for granted that Connel had behaved in a familiar fashion unwelcome to his daughter, and he passed sentence accordingly.

He pulled a case from his pocket, extracted a roll of notes and handed them to Pat.

"You're dismissed from the firm, Connel. This will pay your fare back to England. You can leave in the morning."

"I see," said Pat slowly, and mechanically his fingers closed round the roll of notes. He felt dazed, barely conscious that his world was crumbling to ruins around him. Sonia began to cry hysterically.

"You can't dismiss him . . . I tell you I was to blame as much as he was . . . Daddy . ., listen to me. . . ."

"Don't talk rubbish. How could you be as much to blame?" Mr. Royale thundered in upon her explanations. "At any rate I won't have him come with us one inch farther. He can go back to London and cool his heels. Come along in, Sonia."

She was drawn into the hotel protesting. Pat looked after her, his eyes dark and smouldering. In a way he wished that at this particular juncture of affairs they could

76

have both told John Royale that they loved each other. But obviously it was not a tactful moment for confession. The old man would most certainly have cut up rough and denied them his blessing. But now what? He was disgraced and dismissed and the whole lovely, exciting journey with Sonia was ended.

He found himself confronted by Jane Daunt, Jane whose small face was as pale and set as his own.

"Hullo," he said dully, "are you in on this?"

"I was with Uncle John. Yes. We both saw you. Oh, you fool, Pat, you *fool*! Why do you take such risks?"

"Why do men ever take risks? Because they think them worth while, I suppose."

"Why kiss her good night in full view of the public?"

"I daresay it was mad, but there it is."

Jane beat one small fist on the other.

"It was all so unnecessary, and now you've lost your job!"

"It's pretty grim. But it would be worse if I'd lost Sonia."

Jane made a gesture of exasperation.

"What do you think you're doing, Pat Connel? How do you think all this is going to end? I knew it would only be a question of time before Uncle John found you two out—"

"He hasn't found us out," interrupted Pat. "He's just taken it for granted that I was attempting to be familiar with his daughter, and he won't accept her excuses for me, that's all."

"And how do you think he'd have reacted if you'd come forward with the announcement that your intentions were 'strictly honourable'?" Jane found herself asking with unusual bitterness.

Pat gave a short laugh.

"He'd have told me to go to hell, I daresay, and Sonia

not to make a fool of herself. Perhaps she *is* making a fool of herself, falling for me."

"Perhaps you are the fool?" flashed Jane. "You make me sick and tired . . . both of you."

He stared at her. He had never seen Jane's soft brown eyes flash so furiously before. There was a kind of beauty in her angry young face which also struck him at that moment. Then he laughed again.

"My dear little Jane Daunt, I don't know why you should be so cross."

"Because you've made a mess of things."

"Temporarily, I admit it. But I'm not done—just because I've been sacked. I shall see Sonia before I go and—"

"And what good will that do you?"

"All the good in the world," he said softly. "So long as I know she still cares for me. And I know she does. She was marvellous—trying to take the blame to-night— but the old man was in such a rage it didn't work, and things would have been a bit worse if I'd done the 'intentions are honourable' business."

Jane set her teeth. She almost hated Sonia in this hour and hated Pat, too. This position of knowing everything and being able to say nothing was growing more bitter and difficult every day. She made a movement to pass Pat and go into the hotel. He gripped her arm.

"Don't you think Sonia really loves me, Jane?"

"Find that out for yourself," she flashed, and like a little whirlwind was gone, leaving him gaping after her.

Mr. Royale was still an angry and harassed man when Jane met him in the lounge.

"Here's a nice kettle of fish!" he said. "And the last person I'd have thought would behave in that fashion was Connel."

"And what are we going to do without a chauffeur?" asked Jane, feeling suddenly cold and tired.

"God knows. It's spoilt the whole trip. But I'm not going to have Connel with us. And I'd rather drive myself than engage one of these Spanish devils. Sonia's been making all sorts of excuses for the fellow, but I'd rather not hear them. If she *did* encourage such familiarity, she's a damned little fool and not what I always believed her to be. Personally I think she's just trying to excuse Connel because she's sorry for him. And I don't care if he did lose his head in the moonlight and that rubbish—chauffeurs are not supposed to lose their heads! Pah!"

He walked away from his niece, wiping the moisture from his forehead with a large pocket handkerchief.

Jane went upstairs. She found her cousin in her bedroom. Sonia had ceased weeping. With a sullen, tear-stained face she regarded Jane.

"Well!" she said.

"Well," said Jane, "I hope you're satisfied."

"If you're going to start lecturing me you can get out."

"All right," said Jane. "I'll get out," and she moved toward the communicating-door.

Tears of self-pity sprang to Sonia's eyes again. She rushed after her cousin.

"No, don't go, stay and talk to me. Oh, Janie darling, I wish I'd never been born."

Jane turned and gave her a long disdainful look.

"My dear Sonia, I wonder how many times you say that, and yet you're luckier than millions of women in this world."

"Lucky!" repeated Sonia hysterically, "and what sort of break have I had recently?"

"You've always done what you wanted."

Sonia stamped her foot.

"Well, I didn't want *this* to happen," she said, and covered her face with her hands.

Jane felt suddenly cold. The whole affair was so obnoxious to her that she wished she could walk out of this hotel, become disembodied, and be wafted away somewhere into space up there with those large, clear stars. She was tired of loving hopelessly so much, giving so much and getting so little in return. Yet here was Sonia weeping noisily because she received everything and gave nothing that did not suit her.

"Why, why had Daddy got to come back just at that moment?" Sonia sobbed. "I didn't even know he'd gone out. I thought you were working."

"And what right had you to take Pat out and let him run such a risk? He's lost his job—everything. And you're supposed to love him."

Sonia flung herself face downwards on her bed.

"It's all very well for you. You're a strong fine character and I'm not, that's all. You may find it easy to be so noble, but I don't."

"Oh, Sonia," said Jane. "You're so wrong. I'm not fine and I'm not strong and I don't find it easy to be noble, but I think if I loved a man like Pat Connel I'd try to consider him as well as myself."

Sonia raised a disfigured face.

"What can I do now? I don't want Pat to go back to England. I want to go on seeing him. Oh, I'm so unhappy!"

"But where's it going to end? How can you go on like this, Sonia? You can't play with a man like Pat Connel. I swear you can't."

And the old arguments and protests followed until late that night. They left Jane miserable, tormented with doubts and fears for *him*. They left Sonia with but one

80

idea . . . and that was to prevent her thrilling, delirious love affair from coming to a speedy end.

CHAPTER TEN

SONIA rose early and went round to the garage before anybody else was about. She found Pat standing by the car dressed in tweeds instead of the accustomed uniform. He looked pale and tired, as though he had not slept. But when he saw her his face became transfigured.

"Darling! I knew you'd come."

She rushed into his arms. He gave a deep sigh and let his cheek rest against her head. She was as brilliant and beautiful as the sunlit Spanish morning, he thought, and the warmth of her in his embrace was thrilling and comforting.

"What an awful night I've had!" she said. "I hardly closed my eyes."

"Same here, sweetheart. It was confounded bad luck those two turning up when they did."

"It was my mistake. I thought Daddy was in the hotel. I never dreamed he'd go out."

"I told you when we were sitting in that café I was afraid we'd get found out sooner or later, Sonia. And I don't think I'd have minded if we could have explained the whole position. But it obviously wasn't the moment to do so."

Sonia tightened her arms about him.

"You've never spoken a truer word, my dear. I think if we'd told Daddy last night that we were in love with each other, he'd have exploded. As it was, every time I tried to say that I'd led you on, he shut me up. At one point he said if it *was* true I ought to be thoroughly ashamed of myself."

Pat released her. He lit a cigarette and smoked it in silence for an instance, his face hardening.

"Which only shows that I'm not playing fair," he said. "I ought not to let you carry on like this. The Chief'll never consent to our marriage and I'll never have the right to ask you to leave everything for me."

That was a discussion which Sonia wished to avoid. The future did not concern her so vastly as the present. In her excitable, feckless fashion she lived for the day. She wanted Pat now, and now she must have him. She threw herself back into his arms.

"You're wrong about that. I'm not going to even allow you to get qualms. When we get back to England I can manage Daddy—talk him round. Only we can't spring it on him. It wants very careful slow manoeuvring. Last night has proved that. But you can't stop loving me . . . you *can't*."

He kissed her passionately on lips and throat.

"I know I can't, my sweet. I know it. But it's all gone wrong . . . and I don't quite see . . ."

"We must just go on loving each other!" she broke in breathlessly. "Oh, darling, you *can't* go back to England. I shall loathe every minute of the holiday without you. It will be too dreary for words with just Daddy and Jane."

He looked at her intently.

"Darling Sonia, do you really love me so much?"

She closed her eyes and swore that she did.

"I'll never leave you so long as you want me," he added. "But I've got the sack. I don't quite see what next I'm going to do."

She sighed.

"But what shall we do without you? Daddy's quite a good driver, but as you know, it was my uncle who's dead who designed the Victor, and Daddy knows nothing about the mechanism of it. He doesn't understand the inside of the car like you do, and if things went wrong we'd be stranded."

The thought of the Royales being stranded on some lonely foreign road was not too good. Pat caressed the fair silky head of his beloved and pictured a thousand awful things happening to her. It was typical of him when he said:

"Then I shall not go back to London. I shall follow you."

Sonia was thrilled.

"*Darling*, how can you?"

"Somehow or other. I know the route you're taking. I've studied it for hours. Somewhere in this city there must be a British motor-bike, or an old car. I've got enough money to buy something that will go, and even if I can't keep up with the Victor, I can trail along and eventually catch up with you. The Chief needn't know. I'll follow and keep out of sight."

"Pat, you're marvellous! What a marvellous idea!"

He kissed her on the lips.

"There isn't anything I won't do for you."

Sonia left that garage a good deal more contented than when she had entered it. And Pat went forth into the town prepared to spend the money that had been given him for his fare back to England on anything with two or four wheels that would go. He could imagine Jane Daunt calling him a fool. No doubt he was one. But when a man was in love and his lady loved him, what wouldn't he do for her sake?

Sonia said nothing to Jane when she returned to the hotel. Jane questioned her about Pat and Sonia answered guardedly:

"He hasn't made any definite plans."

For Jane, therefore, the whole trip was spoilt once they moved away from Madrid and traversed the route to Seville. For Jane the sun ceased to shine, the skies were no longer blue, and Spain became the dreariest place in the world. She sat alone in the back of the car and looked wretchedly at Sonia and her father, whose portly figure replaced the familiar handsome one of Connel in his olive-green uniform.

She wondered what on earth Pat meant to do when he got back to London, and how he would get a job without a reference, for of course Uncle John would not give him one. All Uncle John would say about Connel was that it was a catastrophe that he had ever taken the place of the trustworthy Woodham.

Every now and then Sonia turned her head and looked behind her as though expecting to see Pat following in the distance. And whenever Jane caught sight of that pretty, vivid face, she puzzled over it. She wondered just why Sonia appeared so full of suppressed excitement. She felt uneasy. She did not trust Sonia, and one never knew what Pat Connel was going to do next.

They drove without mishap for about one hundred and eighteen kilometres on the road to Seville. Some of the scenery was uninspired straight, monotonous roads flanked by brown, twisted cork trees and the dusty grey of olives. But later they came to a marvellous range of mountains, and the silver River Tajo winding through the valleys.

It was when they were climbing the Puerto de Miravete that the Victor suddenly misbehaved itself and the engine spat and stopped dead. Mr. Royale put on all the brakes and drew the car in to the side of the road.

"Confound it!" he said.

"What is it, Daddy?" asked Sonia.

"I don't know, but it's a damned nuisance stopping like

this just on a hairpin bend and up this damned mountain."

The two girls descended from the car and stretched their limbs while Mr. Royale lifted the bonnet of the car. The sun was setting. The view down the mountain-side and into the valley was dazzling and splendid. But it was Spain at her most rugged and lonely, and not at all the right place for a breakdown.

Sonia and Jane exchanged glances.

"I knew this would happen the moment Daddy took over the wheel," Sonia said in a low voice.

"It'll be fine if we get left here for the night," said Jane drily.

Sonia looked anxiously down the steep road up which they had been climbing.

For the first time she began to feel nervous and strained. She wondered whether Pat was, indeed, following and would eventually reach them. Perhaps he hadn't been able to procure a vehicle. Perhaps he hadn't meant to come. It had been a crazy idea, anyhow.

Mr. Royale was fuming and swearing.

"I can't see what's wrong. Must be autovac trouble, I think. The petrol's not getting through."

Jane went to his side.

"I'm a good secretary, Uncle John, but I don't know anything about motor-cars, unfortunately. Can't we stop somebody?"

"But we don't speak Spanish, my dear girl."

"We might find somebody who understands English."

"And we might not! Be damned to that fellow Connel for his behaviour. He's got us into this mess."

Sonia stood by with downcast eyes and said nothing. Jane thought:

"If only Pat were here!"

A motor-bus came along. The driver was Spanish and

all the people in it were of Spain. They stopped when they saw the big grey car and the trio of English tourists. They gathered round in their friendly fashion, babbled, gesticulated, understood nothing that Mr. Royale tried to say to them, and in the end climbed back into their bus and departed, shrugging their shoulders.

Mr. Royale mopped his forehead, scarlet and furious.

"You oughtn't to have sacked Connel, Daddy," Sonia said in a sweet, faintly malicious voice.

"Don't talk rubbish!" he snapped. "After what he did, how could I possibly have kept him?"

Sonia bit her red lips and said nothing.

The sun was rapidly disappearing behind the mountains. In another half-hour the heat of the day would be gone and the sudden chill of the spring night would descend upon them. The prospect of being hung up for hours and hours without much food, on the Puerto de Miravete was not to be relished by any of them.

And then came a sound for which Sonia had been listening and hoping all day. The honk-honk-honk of a British horn and a quick chug-chug-chug that could belong to nothing but a motor-bike. Eagerly she looked down the road. And yes, into view came a man on a motor-cycle leaving a trail of white dust behind him. Sonia knew, long before the features of the rider were discernible, that it was Pat.

Mr. Royale also watched the approaching vehicle. He said:

"The first motor-bike I've seen in Spain. It must be an Englishman."

Jane, her heart leaping, recognised the rider in spite of a strange check-cap, obviously of Spanish make, and a pair of goggles.

"It's Pat Connel!" she said impulsively.

"Connel!" repeated Mr. Royale, after which he remained speechless.

Thus Pat came back into his own. He had by no means expected to overtake the Victor. But then he had not expected anything so lucky to befall him as a breakdown of the Victor. He had been frankly dubious about the whole situation when he had first left Madrid on this disreputable old Sunbeam, which he had found for sale in an English garage. A little tinkering and it had been made roadworthy, but how long it would remain so he dared not think.

Without wondering what sort of reception he was going to get from the Chief, he pulled the motor-bike up beside the Victor, stepped from it and removed cap and goggles. His first glance was for Sonia, the next for Jane. His eyes twinkled at her. She flushed almost angrily and turned away. Pat saluted Mr. Royale.

"Can I be of any assistance, sir?" he asked with the utmost formality.

Mr. Royale gulped.

"What the devil are you doing here?"

"I just thought I might be of service, sir. I didn't like letting you all go on by yourselves and so I hope you'll forgive me, sir, but I bought this bike and followed."

Mr. Royale passed a handkerchief over his lips. He returned the young man's smiling gaze indignantly.

"The devil you did!" he said.

"Well, Daddy," said Sonia. "It's a terribly good thing he *did*. Now Connel will be able to see what's wrong with the car."

"He shan't touch it!" began Mr. Royale, but Sonia ran and clasped his arm.

"Don't be an idiot, Daddy," she whispered. "We don't want to be stuck here all night. And after all, I think it was marvellous of Connel to follow and not desert us."

"After what he did—" began Mr. Royale.

"I keep telling you," she interrupted, "it was as much my fault as Connel's. And he was dreadfully sorry the next morning—weren't you, Connel?"

"Terribly, sir," said Pat seriously. "Even if you chuck me out at the next town, I hope you'll let me help you now."

Mr. Royale was tired, worried, and longing for a drink. Against all his principles he caved in weakly. And he was a good deal more relieved than he intended to show, that the young puppy had had the audacity to follow them like this.

"Oh, very well," he said. "Get on with it, Connel, and see what's the matter."

Jane caught Pat's gaze again. Those vivid blue eyes of his were wickedly triumphant. He actually winked at her before he moved to the side of the Victor and began an examination of the engine. Jane pursed her lips.

"So *this* is what they arranged," she thought. "And this is why Sonia kept looking over her shoulder. She expected him!"

She refused to confess even to herself that she was thoroughly glad to see Pat again. Her pleasure would soon have evaporated before that look on Sonia's face. She had got what she wanted and was ill-disguising her feelings. Jane turned away from the pair of them feeling absolutely defeated. It was all such madness. Last night's disaster had not taught them a lesson. Other disasters would follow—she knew it.

Mr. Royale took his daughter's arm and walked her firmly down the road.

"I'm feeling stiff and a few steps will do us both good, my dear," he said. "Come along."

Sonia could not refuse. She knew perfectly well that her father was going to keep her well away from Connel even if he remained with them. But remain he must. She wheedled Mr. Royale in her most beguiling fashion.

"You must let Connel take us on to Seville, or even farther. Dismissing him that way was a mistake, Daddy."

"No mistake at all!" exploded Mr. Royale. "I can't have the man who acts as my chauffeur kissing my daughter in that familiar fashion . . . good heavens, what next? I don't care if the fellow *is* as well educated as we are."

"Spanish moons are very glamorous, Daddy," said Sonia in her silkiest voice, and rubbed her beautiful head against his shoulder. "And I'm *so* attractive, aren't I?"

"Attractive!" echoed Mr. Royale with a snort. "I think you're a baggage."

"What a lovely Victorian word, Daddy!"

"But seriously, Sonia, you don't want me to believe that you're on such terms with young Connel, do you?"

She bit her lip and crimsoned.

"I don't know what you mean by 'on such terms,' but he's a very nice young man, isn't he? You've always said so."

Mr. Royale became suddenly profoundly shocked and worried.

"Sonia, you're not suggesting . . ."

"Oh, Daddy, you're taking it all too solemnly," she broke in, terrified to pursue the conversation.

"My darling little girl," he said, "you're all I have. All I've had since your mother died. I've always wanted you to be happy, but at the same time, when you get married I want it to be to a man worthy of you. You have so much to offer . . . your beauty, your youth, my money when I'm gone. You could marry anybody. But it must be Somebody with a capital S."

She remained silent. Her heart was sinking very low. Pat Connel was not, in Mr. Royale's estimation, Somebody with a capital S. And as for Maurice, God . . . this discussion had only made her all the more aware that she dared not tell him the truth.

"Why discuss my marriage? It has nothing to do with Connel," she said as lightly as possible. "Take my advice, and forget that stupid incident last night, and take Connel on again. We'll never manage to drive through Morocco without him. Give him another chance."

"Then for heaven's sake, Sonia, be more decorous and see that Connel keeps his place."

While this argument was in progress, Jane stood watching Pat, who by now had the carburettor in pieces.

"Well," she said, "I suppose you think you've been very clever."

He glanced up at her.

"Don't be cross with me, little Jane Daunt. You were so very furious last night."

"I am—still."

"Because I followed?"

"Oh, because of so many things!" she said in a voice of exasperation.

"You don't like me any more, do you?"

Jane's dark eyes turned to the scarlet glow of the sun behind the sombre Spanish mountains. She felt suddenly cold and tired and annoyed with herself because she knew that she was glad, so much too glad to see this handsome impetuous young man who was unconsciously drawing ruin down upon himself.

If only she could have said to him:

"Follow us, do what you like, only *don't* pin your faith on Sonia or you will be hurt!"

But she could say nothing. So Pat took it for granted that he had lost some of that friendship which she had always given him in London. He was sorry because he admired Jane Daunt. He even had a curious kind of affection for her.

He returned to his work.

"I had the hell's own journey pursuing you," he said. "And I didn't dare stop for a meal in case I should never catch you up. But a motor-bike in the hot sunshine and dust after the comfort of the Victor . . . ye gods . . . can't you imagine it?"

She could, and she suddenly noticed that his face was livid with fatigue and streaked with grime. His forehead was drenched with perspiration.

"Look here," she said. "You're all in. Take a minute's rest and I'll give you a sip of tea from my flask."

He wiped his forehead and grinned at her.

"That's decent of you. You're always very nice to me really, although you don't approve of me."

The way he smiled down at her seemed to break her heart. Raw with pain she snapped at him:

"Oh, shut up! Sit down on the running-board and drink some tea."

But he refused to do anything until he had put the car in working order. It was a very small thing that was wrong and he soon found it. Suddenly the silence of the mountain road was broken by the deep-throated hum of the big Victor engine. A sound very welcome to Mr. Royale who heard it and came hurrying back with Sonia. Then, quite suddenly, Pat collapsed. He sat down on the running-board of the car. His head fell back.

"Want . . . food. . . ." he gasped heavily. "Sorry to be such a fool. . . ."

All that was tender in Jane surged to the surface. She forgot everybody else but Pat. In a moment she was at his side with a thermos of tea and some sandwiches from the luncheon basket which they had taken from Madrid. She could see that Pat was near to fainting. She put an arm about his shoulders and with her own handkerchief wiped his face, then lifted a cup of tea to his lips. He drank thirstily.

"That's . . . grand!"

Sonia, frightened at what she saw, rushed up.

"Oh . . . are you ill?"

Jane immediately moved away from Pat and made furious signs to Sonia to be quiet.

"Ssh . . . little idiot . . . do you want to give everything away?"

Sonia put a hand to her mouth and stood still. And now Pat's bloodshot eyes turned to her. She looked so beautiful standing there in the light of the setting sun that his heart seemed to melt at the sight of her, and his drooping spirits revived. Jane ceased to exist for him. But it was Jane who came back with more food and made him eat.

Mr. Royale looked on a trifle dubiously.

"Damn silly business doing all those miles on a motor-cycle," he said. "Wonder you didn't kill yourself."

"I nearly did, sir," said Pat and stood up, feeling better after his refreshment.

Sonia gripped her father's arm.

"Go on, Daddy," she whispered. "Take him back. You said you would."

Mr. Royale, still under his daughter's influence, thereupon somewhat pompously announced words of pardon.

"You behaved badly last night, Connel, but on condition you keep in the position you took with us when you came in Woodham's shoes, you may continue with us to Morocco," he said.

Pat, exulting, saluted stiffly.

"Thank you very much indeed, sir."

Jane climbed back into the car feeling helpless and hopeless.

Mr. Royale, however, saw to it that Sonia sat in the

back of the car with her cousin and that he, himself, took the place beside the prodigal driver.

The motor-bike was abandoned on the roadside. Pat bade farewell to it almost regretfully. It had made almost every bone in his body ache, but at least it had brought him to Sonia's rescue, so he felt a certain attachment for it. However, it was good to be back in the luxurious Victor, and he felt more relieved when they started up the mountain road again.

CHAPTER ELEVEN

Two more days of this journey and they were in Algeciras where they stayed a night at the Hôtel Reina Christina because Mr. Royale wished to make notes on the ruins of a Moorish aqueduct and take photographs of Ayuntamiento, where the Pact of Algeciras had been signed in 1906.

By this time he was quite restored to his good humour and had reinstated Connel into favour. The young man was invaluable. He had to admit it. And except for that one lapse had not shown further familiarity in his behaviour toward Sonia. He was formality itself. Neither had Mr. Royale further cause to feel uneasy about Sonia's attitude where Connel was concerned. She was obviously "putting him in his place". That Madrid affair was nothing to worry about.

They motored from Algeciras into Gibraltar, and thence journeyed by boat to Tangier.

As the boat moved away from Gibraltar Jane leaned over the rails and watched the mighty Rock gradually fade into the distance. She had left her uncle and cousin, feeling unlike Sonia's chatter, and relieved for half an hour of taking the incessant notes from her uncle. She felt solitary. She wanted to be alone. At the other end of the deck she could discern Pat's uniformed figure.

She felt a sudden loathing of the whole situation, and a curious growing distaste at the prospect of the weeks ahead of her in Morocco. Yet it was all wonderful. Everything around her was new and wonderful, full of vivid colour and romance. More than anything on earth she wanted to be with Pat Connel, and equally, under these circumstances, preferred not to be. She was so utterly removed from him.

They were passing so close to the coast that she could see the little Spanish farms nestling against the hillsides. The sea was blue-green, shimmering in the sunlight. Soon they were to leave Tarifa, the last port of Spain, behind them, and come to North Africa, where the rising mountains looked dark and sinister against a sky of purest blue.

The wind blew fresher and colder and now the mountains rose so high that the peaks were wreathed in the curling vapours. Over those mountains lay Tetuan and Pogador to which they would be journeying by car tomorrow.

Jane's gaze turned from the scenery toward Pat. He, too, was leaning over the rails staring beyond him, a cigarette in the corner of his mouth. She wondered if he was enjoying it as much as she. She would like to have gone to his side and talked to him. But she stayed where she was with that curious depression weighing down her heart.

Then suddenly even her enjoyment in the scenery was taken from her and her peace rudely shattered. She saw Sonia coming quickly toward her. Sonia with a chalk-white face and fear staring from her eyes.

"My dear, what on earth has happened?"

94

Sonia clutched her arm. Her teeth were chattering.

"Jane! Jane, something *awful!*"

"What?"

Jane had to put an arm around her because the girl was swaying, all her beauty wiped out by a ghastly look of terror. She had never seen Sonia look like that before.

"Tell me what's happened, quickly...."

Sonia found her voice.

"Maurice," she said. "*Maurice....*"

The colour rushed to Jane's cheeks.

"Maurice! Do you mean he's *here*, that you've seen him?"

"Yes. And he's seen me. Look ... I've just rushed away from Daddy to you ... *look!*"

Jane looked. And her own heart seemed to stand still. She saw a slightly built man who wore a black beret, French fashion, on the side of a fair head. The slim figure, just a shade too debonair, in a pin-striped suit and light check travelling coat, was all too familiar to Jane. It was Maurice Gardener, all right. Sonia's husband. Jane stared at him stupefied.

"What in the name of heaven is he doing here? Is he alone? Have you seen anyone with him?"

"No, he seems to be quite alone," said Sonia in a trembling voice. "Oh, my God, I suppose he's travelling, like we are, but why he should have chosen to come to Tangier at the same time as ourselves and be on *our boat*, I can't imagine! It's just a coincidence and the most appalling piece of bad luck for me!"

"Pull yourself together, and leave things to me," Jane said in her decisive manner.

"But what are we going to do?" wailed Sonia.

"Let me talk to him," said Jane.

But there was no chance for her to say anything to Maurice Gardener alone. At that precise moment he had turned and strolled along the deck to the two girls. Sonia was clinging on to Jane's arm in abject fear. The man's gaze fell upon them. His slightly bored expression altered to one of extreme interest and astonishment. The next minute he was there before them, sweeping off his beret with exaggerated courtesy.

"Hey! Of all the astonishing things. Sonia! And Cousin Jane!"

Sonia was incapable of answering. It seemed hard to her now to believe that she had ever fallen in love with Maurice. Much harder to credit that she had been fool enough to marry him. He was good-looking, yes. He had a gay, pleasant voice with the slightest foreign inflection. And she could remember that he had always made love divinely. But that she should have *married* him . . . heavens!

Jane did not lose her head. She said:

"Well, Maurice, you are the last person we expected to see."

"The world is full of lovely surprises," he said, and added with a swift look of appreciation at the beautiful soignée figure of his wife . . . "And Sonia is surely the loveliest surprise of all."

Sonia remained mute. Said Jane drily:

"Don't let's waste time exchanging compliments. Are you staying in Tangier?"

He replaced his beret. His white teeth flashed in a smile.

"Surely! I'm on a little health trip. I've had a severe chill which almost turned to pneumonia, and in Paris the winds have been cold. My doctor ordered sunlight, and in Morocco I hope to find it. But I hope to find something even more delightful now that I've met you."

"What do you want, Maurice?" Sonia suddenly asked in a sharp frightened voice.

"It would take far too long for me to tell you that in detail," he smiled.

Sonia drew a sharp breath and looked in the direction of the glass loggia. Her father was still sitting there placidly smoking his cigar. But the sight of him struck fresh fear in her heart.

"Is it more money you want?" she whispered.

"Sonia, leave it to me," said Jane. "Maurice has had quite enough out of you. Why don't you go back to Uncle John and let me deal with this?"

Then Maurice coolly put his arm through Sonia's. He smiled at Jane, but the smile was defiant.

"I'm not so sure that I wish to be dealt with by you, little Cousin Jane. You interfered in Paris and broke things up between Sonia and me, and I'd rather not be interfered with any more."

Jane flushed.

"You wonder that I interfere? Did you expect me to go back to London and leave Sonia with you, after what she found out?"

Sonia looked round her wildly.

"Oh, be quiet, both of you. Somebody will hear!"

Maurice patted her hand.

"Nobody's going to hear, my dear. And don't be so foolish. I won't give you away if that's what you are afraid of. Nothing would give me greater pleasure than to announce to the whole boat that you are Mrs. Maurice Gardener. You are so chic—so good-looking. I always did think you were one of the loveliest girls I ever met. However . . ."

"You really mean you won't give me away?" she said hysterically.

"Not for the moment, anyhow."

"Then it is more money you want!"

"My dear child, I admit that one has to live," he

97

drawled. "What you have been sending me lately hasn't been altogether adequate. And you know I lost my job at Christmas. I have been spending capital. If it hadn't been for your . . . shall we put it as kindness . . . I'd have had a bad time. Still, the old firm's taken me back now. So I'm not so hard hit. As a matter of fact I was going to write to you, Sonia, and ask you to meet me and talk things over."

She snatched her hand away from his. She was calmer now. Full of distaste she regarded him.

"What is there to talk about? Unless you're willing to set me free . . . let me divorce you. You refused to do so in Paris. You said you'd given up that other girl and that I couldn't find any evidence against you. That's why things have remained as they are. And of course I know perfectly well why. You prefer to keep me tied to you knowing that I shall never dare tell my father, and to get as much money out of me as you can! Oh, I despise you. . . !"

She broke off, panting.

"Sonia dear, don't get all worked up again," said Jane. "Much better to keep calm about it."

Maurice extracted a cigarette from a packet and lit it.

"Can't we dispense with the *duenna*?" he said. "I think it would be tactful if she left husband and wife to have a word together, alone."

Sonia turned pale at the words. But she said:

"Oh, all right. If you want to see me alone . . . perhaps it is better, Jane."

Jane shrugged her shoulders. She was quite sick and tired of dragging Sonia out of difficulties. She had no desire whatsoever to remain. But she wondered what was at the back of Maurice Gardener's brain.

She could see Pat, still leaning up against the rails, enjoying the stern beauty of the mountains outlined against the gentian sky. Poor Pat! What disillusionment lay in store for him! Jane wondered what he would say if he knew that his idolised and idealised Sonia was now in conversation with *her husband*.

Sonia, in a panic, drew Maurice away to the farthest end of the boat, where she hoped she could not be seen by father or lover.

"Now, for God's sake tell me what you want, Maurice," she said.

"Who are you so nervous of? The old man . . . ?"

She bit her lip. Maurice gave a low amused laugh.

"Don't tell me you've fallen for somebody else."

"You wouldn't have a right to criticize me if I have."

"Tut, tut, *cherie*, a husband's rights. . . ."

The French word of endearment brought the colour blazing to her cheeks. He had always called her *cherie*. Once she had thought it so sweet a word! How dead indeed is a dead love!

"You have no rights over me," she said. "And anyhow, even if you have, you swore you'd leave me alone as long as you got the money."

He shrugged his shoulders.

"This is all so crude! Let us be a little more delicate about it. Whether you believe me or not, I am not quite the mercenary fellow you think. I am human—with human impulses. Once I was very much in love . . ."

"With my money!" she cut in. "And my position as John Royale's daughter."

"I don't agree."

"I saw it in black and white in that letter to Colette. You told her that you loved her and that you married me entirely for my money."

"It wasn't altogether true, Sonia. I swear it. Colette was

99

a little devil with a fiendish temper and I had to conciliate her somehow."

"That's a lie. And anyhow I don't see the use of raking up the past. Things were said which you can't deny and I told you I'd never willingly see you again."

He looked down at her. He had half forgotten that gold-and-white loveliness of hers. Perhaps in the first place he had never really loved her. He was a born gambler and it was a gambler's instinct which had made him elope with John Royale's daughter. He had made a muck of it. He had made a muck of that Colette business. But now he was not sure that he wouldn't like to settle down and be a good husband to lovely Sonia.

"Listen, *cherie*," he said. "Don't be so bitter against me. Perhaps we both of us made mistakes, but it is never too late to mend."

"My dear Maurice, if you are trying to effect a touching reconciliation, you are making the biggest mistake of your life."

"Then you are in love with somebody else," he said.

She thought of Pat. And suddenly she said between her teeth:

"Yes, I am. What of it?"

"Oh, come!" he said, smiling, "I can't allow infidelity, it would be too heart-breaking!"

"For God's sake stop being flippant, and tell me what you want."

"That touching reconciliation which you speak of," he said coolly.

She stared at him in blank dismay. If he had wanted money she might have got some more for him. But he wanted *her*, that was very different.

"I really can't bear to see you look so unhappy," he added. "So don't let's talk about it any more. Where are you staying in Tangier?"

"El Minza," she said hopelessly.

"I, also."

"You're going to follow me?"

"Not at all. It is where I intended to stay. You will see my luggage is labelled. And you need not be afraid that I shall give away anything. If you are nice to me, I won't —for the moment, anyhow."

That sounded sinister to her. She said:

"Daddy knows you well enough, and he's bound to think it most peculiar, you being on the scene."

"My dear child, that's absurd. I've just as much right to stay at El Minza as you and your father. Now don't worry. I haven't the slightest desire to do you any harm, so take that frightened look off your lovely face. And here comes Cousin Jane in hot pursuit of us. So perhaps you'd better run along. We'll have a word to-night in the hotel."

Sonia turned away. She realised that there was nothing further to say at the moment. But her spirits were very low when she joined her cousin.

Sonia repeated the conversation.

"It's simply frightful," she said. "There is no question of us being reconciled. I hate him, and I love Pat. Jane, Jane, it's such a mess . . . and I don't know what to do."

Jane had little advice to offer. It was useless going over all the old ground. Useless pleading with Sonia to tell her father the truth and to give Pat a square deal. But if Maurice Gardener was to stay at their hotel and was going to assert himself, there was nothing so far as Jane could see to avert calamity.

CHAPTER TWELVE

In the Moorish court of the Hôtel El Minza, Jane sat alone smoking a cigarette and thinking about bed. She was tired after the day's journey and the strong sea air made her sleepy.

She decided regretfully that it would be a waste of time to go to bed and sleep, and waste of a glorious night. She had thought that nothing could be lovelier than the nights in Spain. But Morocco was unimaginably lovely. The whole place was like a tale from the *Arabian Nights*. Tangier, a fairy city with its white walls and slits of windows, its slender towers and minarets flooded in a splendour of moonlight.

Beauty and romance walked hand in hand in this place, and all that was romantic awoke in Jane's heart to-night. She was not ashamed of her emotions. She was as frank with herself as with others. She knew that she was tired of being practical and calm and efficient; tired of helping Sonia out of troubles and of typewriting Uncle John's dull notes. She wanted love and a lover . . . *the* lover. That meant, of course, that she wanted Pat.

Much as she appreciated this journey and, in particular this enchanting Morocco, she really dreaded the rest of the trip. It wasn't easy to be so near Pat day by day and to watch him wasting his time and affections on Sonia. It was an acute irritation. Deeper than that, it was sheer pain.

What a day it had been!

Uncle John had disliked the arrival at Tangier; the hideous upheaval on the quay, with masses of Arabs swarming, screaming, jostling. There had been feverish scenes in the custom house, lengthy examinations of the car, of the luggage; all the paraphernalia which wasted over an hour before the gates of Morocco were flung open to receive the battered travellers and their even more battered possessions.

It had amused Jane, but Uncle John preferred something more British and orderly. Pat had been a great help with his knowledge of Spanish. But Pat was not himself. He was depressed because he had not seen Sonia alone for a long while. And Sonia was even more depressed with the shadow of Maurice Gardener in the background.

Of course Maurice had to come face to face with the Royale party sooner or later and they met him in the lounge just before dinner. He passed by without any more recognition than a faint smile and nod at Sonia.

Where Sonia was just now Jane had no idea. She presumed the foolish girl was indulging in one of her dangerous assignations with Pat.

She soon discovered that she was wrong on that score, for Pat himself made an appearance in the Moorish court, Pat in grey flannels looking worried and unhappy and obviously searching for somebody. Jane watched him make a nervous investigation of the various tables in and out the arches, then she called in a low voice:

"Pat!"

He hurried toward her. He seemed glad to see her.

"Hullo, Jane. Where's Sonia?"

She did not answer for a moment. But she thought with some bitterness what a little fool she was to have sat here in a state of romantic glamour thinking about this man whose first words to her were of desire for another woman.

"Where is Sonia?" he repeated.

"I don't know. I imagined she was with you."

"And where's the Chief? Dare I stay and yarn with you for a second?"

"If you want to. Uncle John's gone to bed."

Pat balanced himself on the arm of a basket-chair, hands thrust in his pockets, handsome face moody.

"I haven't had a chance to say a word to Sonia all day."

"Just as well."

"You would say that, of course. You don't realise how much we love each other."

"I realise quite how much *you* love *her*!"

Pat's chin shot up.

"Are you suggesting that she doesn't love me just as much?"

Jane flung away her cigarette.

"My dear Pat, I don't want to suggest anything. I don't really want to talk about it at all."

"Sorry if it bores you," he said huffily.

He was so like a spoiled little boy, she longed to put her arms around him in that moment and draw that attractive head close to her breast and tell him what a darling fool he was and how much she adored him. Instead of which, she said:

"Well, it is a bit boring . . . after a time. I've had it the whole trip."

His expression changed. He smiled at her. Little Jane was looking rather nice to-night, he thought, in her thin chiffon dress of palest yellow, with a black embroidered Spanish shawl over one shoulder. It made her face look piquant and vivid. She was utterly different to Sonia, and Pat's head was usually much too full of Sonia to think about Jane's physical attractions. But to-night suddenly he noticed them. He said:

"I daresay it bores you to death, Jane. And you've been damn good to both of us. Don't let's discuss her or myself. After all it's my own tangle and I've got to unwind it as best I can. Only I assure you she does love me, and that she wants just as much as I do for us to get married quickly."

Jane felt suddenly stubborn. She wasn't going to answer that indirect challenge and she wasn't going to put herself out to encourage him or allay his doubts and fears. He offered her a cigarette and she took it. As he lit it his hand touched hers and sent the blood racing through her body.

"How calm and poised you are, little Jane Daunt. I don't think I have ever met a woman so sure of herself."

Jane gave a quick, nervous laugh.

"Sure of myself!" she repeated. "But in what way?"

"Oh, lots of funny little ways. You are such a decisive character."

She laughed again and paid strict attention to her cigarette. This was the first time that Pat Connel had ever talked to her in quite such a personal strain. The first time for many long days, anyhow, that he had found time to discuss anything but Sonia. It was rather pleasant to have him standing here before her, leaning against one of the white arches, taking a sudden interest in her.

"My dear Pat," she said, "you make me sound as though I were a prim and prudish school-marm briskly conducting classes."

"Not at all. . . ." Pat flicked the ash from his cigarette. The red point glowed in the darkness. "You look much too charming and you *are* much too charming to be a school-marm!"

She felt her cheeks scorch. Flattery from Pat! Heavens, what next? But it made her almost angry. She was not going to allow herself to be flattered just because Pat flung compliments at her in his facile Irish fashion. She almost snapped:

"Nonsense! That's a worn-out theory. Heaps of school

mistresses these days are most attractive. And anyhow I'm *not* charming."

"Well, I think you've been terribly so—to both Sonia and myself."

Jane grit her teeth. Of course, Sonia must come into this!

"Well, I haven't felt charming," she said. "It's all upset me a lot."

"Now we are getting away from the subject of you."

"Why not?"

"I want to talk about you."

"Believe me, I'm a very dull subject."

"Sure and you're not!" drawled Pat's beguiling voice, and it made her feel suddenly helpless, powerless to put up too much of a fight against him in her heart, however much she fought against him on the surface. There were just times like these when she pitied Sonia from the bottom of her heart. It couldn't be easy for Sonia to relinquish Pat as a lover.

"May I just ask you one thing?" Pat went on.

"What?"

"Have *you* ever been in love?"

She tightened up. She dared not look in his direction. Pitching her half-smoked cigarette into the darkness, she stared after it.

"You don't think that's impertinent of me, do you?" added Pat in an apologetic voice.

Answering him, she managed to make her voice sound casual.

"Not at all, but why does it interest you?"

He sighed.

"I was just wondering whether you knew how these things affect one . . . I mean, really being in love does just eat one up . . . I wondered if you realised what it can be like."

She was silent an instant. She who knew so well that love could become an obsession. Sometimes it seemed to her that she was, indeed, being eaten up with love for Pat.

"That makes love sound a destructive thing," at length she said. "It shouldn't destroy . . . it should inspire and enrich . . ." she broke off abruptly. It was almost more than she could bear to sit here discussing love with Pat.

But he seemed enthusiastic to continue.

"Sure, and that's true, Jane. I agree with you. And I think that love *is* the greatest of all inspirations. But one can be consumed by it."

"One shouldn't allow oneself to be."

"There speaks the practical little Jane. No, I don't think that you have been in love."

She rose with an abrupt movement. Her shawl slid from her shoulder and trailed on the ground. Pat picked it up and placed it round her shoulders.

"You're not cold, are you? Why, you're shivering."

She wondered if he could be more maddening. And how dared he take it for granted that she had not been in love just because she was more in control of herself than he was, perhaps, and certainly more so than Sonia?

She came to the conclusion that if life had horrid little punishments in store for people who gave vent to their feelings, it imposed equal penalties on those who held themselves in check.

"I'm going in," she said. "I think I am a bit chilly."

"I'm sorry," he said, and meant it.

He would have liked to stay talking to Jane. She was a queer, reserved little thing, but he had a profound admiration for her. He knew that Sonia had also. A pity that Jane did not understand much about the "grand passion." He felt that it would soften and improve her.

She was distinctly attractive physically. He had thought, when he had looked down at her just now, what marvellous eyes she had . . . wide-set, brown, velvety. She was not all hard, this little Jane!

Suddenly Pat said:

"Listen! Isn't that Sonia's voice? Is it herself that's coming? Ought I to bolt . . . I mean do you think the Chief will be with her?"

"No. Uncle John went to bed an hour ago."

They stood still together, side by side, half hidden by one of the white arches. Coming through the court toward them was Sonia and a man in evening clothes. To Pat he was a stranger. But Jane recognised that debonair figure and her heart gave a horrid little twist. Maurice! What on earth was Sonia doing with him? They had barely acknowledged each other just before dinner. But Jane knew that Maurice Gardener was not to be trusted. She had wondered ever since they had met on the boat what game he was up to now. Sonia had thought that he was trying to get her back. It looked like it. Jane felt suddenly nervous. It would not do for Pat to meet Maurice. The fat would be in the fire. She touched Pat's arm.

"I shouldn't stay if I were you."

But Pat's blue eyes were gazing in Sonia's direction. He had never seen her look more lovely than to-night in that black lace dinner dress which made her skin appear dazzling white. Her hair was silver fair, and she had put a red flower behind her ear as she had learned to do in Spain. His whole heart seemed to grow molten with love for her. He felt that he *must* see her to say good night, to hold her in his arms before he turned in for the night.

"Wait a second, Jane," he said.

Jane opened her lips to speak, then shut them again. She did not like the situation, but after all it was not her business. And why should she bother to drag Pat away from danger. He had been rushing into it from the first moment that he had declared his love for Sonia. It was his own funeral.

Sonia and Maurice had come to a standstill between the arches at right angles to Jane and Pat. It was obvious that Sonia had not seen them. She was talking very earnestly to Maurice and, although they could not hear what she said, her voice sounded urgent and slightly on the hysterical note.

Decidedly ill-at-ease, Jane glanced at Pat. His brows were knit.

"Who's that fellow with Sonia?"

Jane made no reply.

"I know," added Pat. "I noticed him on the boat coming over. He was wearing a beret. He isn't English, is he?"

Jane maintained silence. She felt quite powerless to answer any questions about Maurice Gardener. But there came across her in that instant a fateful sensation that this was a moment of crisis . . . a big crucial moment in all their lives.

Sonia, still unaware that she was being observed by her lover and her cousin, continued to argue with the man who was her husband.

CHAPTER THIRTEEN

THE whole evening had seemed to Sonia one long argument. Whilst dressing for dinner she had argued with Jane, who had started all that old business about her making a clean breast of things to her father, instead of continuing a lot of lies and deception. Sonia had refused.

During dinner Mr. Royale, noticing Maurice Gardener at a table not far from them, had expressed his contempt of men of Maurice's type and of all spongers, finishing up with an onslaught against any young man who failed to get a job and hold it, and who took money from women. He had no use for them.

Jane, of course, had agreed. She, herself, was independent by nature and hated being beholden to anybody unless she gave something in exchange.

But Sonia, out of sheer perversity, argued in the opposite direction. She had every excuse for a poor fellow who couldn't get work or hadn't a penny, she declared. And why shouldn't he accept help or charity from those who could afford to give it? Where was the disgrace? Of course a hot argument ensued, and Mr. Royale made it quite clear that if ever a young gentleman of that type came after his daughter, he would be sent flying.

After dinner Sonia managed to whisper in Jane's ear:

"There! You see how impossible it would be for me to tell Daddy the truth about Maurice, or even about Pat being in love with me."

But Jane had no sympathy. She answered:

"You may be a coward about Maurice, but that doesn't excuse you for being cowardly about a man you are supposed to love."

Altogether a wretched evening for Sonia, and worse was to follow when, instead of being able to slip off and meet her lover, she was waylaid by Maurice, who insisted upon having a long discussion with her. Then followed the longest and fiercest of the arguments.

At the end of an hour of reproaches, bitterness, pleadings, protests, nothing had been settled between them. But the very fact that Sonia seemed disinclined to renew the old affections and bonds seemed to inflame Maurice to quite a sincere passion for her. A passion, however, which frightened far more than it flattered Sonia.

They had come finally to the Moorish court; Maurice still begging her to reconsider her decisions; Sonia imploring him to go away and leave her alone.

"I'll try and get you more money," she was saying now, raising a pale, distraught face to his. "Only go away, go away, *do*!"

He made an expressive foreign gesture with both hands.

"*Cherie*, you can't dislike me as much as this. Don't you remember our first wonderful night in Paris...."

"And that third wonderful night when I found out what you really were!" she broke in hysterically.

"Couldn't you believe that I am sorry and let us begin again? I have a job, and if you care to live on what I earn, you need not trouble *cher* Papa at all."

"Don't you understand that I haven't the slightest wish to live with you again?"

"So! You must be very much in love with this other man. Who is he?"

"That's my affair."

"Mine also, surely."

"I refuse to stay here talking to you," she said, and turned to leave him.

Pat Connel, watching from the shadows, was then amazed to see the fair-haired man in the dinner jacket catch Sonia by the arm and pull her into his arms. Pat went white to the lips. His cigarette fell from his fingers.

"No, that's too much!" he said under his breath.

Jane, with very little colour in her own cheeks, caught his wrist.

"Wait, Pat. Jealousy is a dangerous thing...."

"But she can't want ..." he began.

Then he heard Sonia's raised voice, every word distinct:

"Cad ... you *mean* cad! Don't touch me...."

That was enough for Pat. He sprang forward, wrenching his wrist away from Jane's small nervous fingers.

"That's enough for me!" he said, between his teeth, and seizing Maurice by the shoulders, dragged him away from Sonia.

"You . . .!"

He never said the other word. But his clenched fist caught Maurice by surprise, a well-aimed blow on the jaw which sent the other man sprawling on the ground.

Sonia looked at him speechlessly. He was the last person she had expected to see. The last one from whom she wanted support at this particular moment. She had an instant of agonising anxiety. What in heaven's name would Maurice do if he turned nasty about this? What would he say? She was to know soon enough.

Maurice had lost his balance, but the blow had not been hard enough to knock him out. He staggered on to his feet and stood there, a hand to his bruised cheek, staring a trifle dazedly at the man who had hit him.

Jane came slowly forward and stood apart from the trio, a tense quiet spectator of this drama. She knew quite well what was going to happen. This was the moment which she had anticipated ever since the affair between Sonia and Pat began. This would be the commencement of the little hell which Pat had unwittingly been storing up for himself.

Maurice spoke to Pat.

"Who the devil are you?"

His face was a mottled crimson. He breathed fast. Pat answered:

"That doesn't matter. But I might put the same question to you. *And* ask why the hell you laid a hand on Miss Royale."

"Wait, Pat . . ." began Sonia frenziedly.

But Maurice cut in.

"Miss Royale, eh? That's amusing. And so you think I have no right to lay a hand on her, do you?"

Pat blinked and stared. The man's significant words and attitude sent a horrible wave of nausea over him.

Maurice continued:

"Since you think I have not the right to touch Miss—er—Royale—perhaps I had better disillusion you as to your own right to knock me down for doing so. My name's Gardener. Maurice Gardener."

"I've never heard of you," rapped out Pat.

Maurice took a silk handkerchief from his pocket and wiped his lips.

"So! Then Sonia has kept very quiet about me."

Sonia stepped forward.

"Maurice!" her voice was full of wild entreaty.

He disregarded it.

"No, I'm not going to be treated like this . . . knocked down by anyone who thinks he has more right to you than I have."

He turned to Pat.

"Look here, young man. Let us make the introduction more thorough. I am Maurice Gardener and Sonia is Mrs. Maurice Gardener. In other words a gentleman has a perfectly good right to kiss his own wife good night."

Jane held her breath. So the truth was out at last! How would Pat take it? Poor Pat. She could pity him now. This was going to be a far bigger blow to him than the physical one he had dealt to the other man. Maurice was well revenged.

Pat stared dazedly first at Maurice and then at Sonia. Then he said:

"Tell me that is a lie."

She could not answer. She was tongue-tied. She looked as though she was going to faint. He seized her arm and shook her roughly.

"Go on! Tell me that man's lying. He *must* be!"

She shook her head wildly. In that moment, Sonia was punished a dozen times over for deceiving Pat Connel. All her weeks of scheming of hoping were being smashed in front of her eyes. She had played a losing game and now she knew it. She was lost.

Maurice said, with a more than usually strong foreign accent:

"Perhaps, *m'sieu*, you are to be excused, since you did not know that Sonia was married—and to me."

Pat ignored him. His gaze was riveted upon Sonia. His fingers still gripped her arm. His eyes looked like blue stones, clear, hard, pitiless.

"You tell me, *you* tell me! . . . Is it true? Are you married to this man?"

She collapsed and would have fallen if Jane had not hurried up and put a strong arm around her.

"Leave her alone, you two great bullies!" Jane said in a low tone. "Leave her alone. You're half killing her."

Sonia burst into tears and was led, or rather dragged, by Jane to a chair, in which she fell. She sat there, crumpled up, her fair head bowed on her arms. The two men looked down at her. Maurice shrugged his shoulders and nursed his injured cheek. He had broken all his promises not to betray Sonia, but after all, he did not relish being knocked down by a total stranger, and if Sonia was playing a double game it was time she was stopped.

But Pat Connel looked at Sonia with very different emotions. The sight of that bowed figure and the sound of her weeping hurt him unbelievably. All her pride and beauty were trailing in the dust. He knew that Maurice Gardener had not lied. Her silence and collapse were definite admissions of guilt. She *was* married to the man. *Married!* God, was it possible?

Pat had thought of her as having admirers, scores of

them. A lover, perhaps. But a husband, never. She had promised to marry him. She had allowed him to build up a hundred wonderful dreams. He felt that she had committed an unforgivable sin in lying to him. All her love had been a lie. She had known all the way along that she could not marry him. She had taken his love only to satisfy her vanity. What an utter, utter fool he had been!

Jane, standing beside Sonia, trying without much success to calm her, looked up and spoke sharply to Maurice.

"You've done enough harm for to-night. Why don't you clear out?"

"*Eh bien*. I'm sorry," he said. "I didn't mean to do this. She drove me to it. Of course I won't say anything to the old man. . . ."

"Oh, go away!" said Jane.

Pat detained Maurice. Very white and set, he said stiffly:

"I apologise for knocking you down. I didn't know . . ."

Maurice put up a deprecating hand.

"But naturally. You have my sympathies. I do not know who you are, but my—er—charming wife is fortunate to have a champion with such a powerful right hand."

He bowed, and with a flashing smile made his exit.

"I almost wish you'd knocked him out for good and all," muttered Jane.

Pat sneered:

"Thanks. I'm not swinging in order to make a widow of Sonia."

Sonia darted up wildly, her face blotched and tear-stained.

"Pat . . . don't . . . don't be too hard . . . if you knew everything. . . ."

"I don't want to know anything," he cut in. "Enough lies have been told."

"Well, I daresay you'll get the truth now," said Jane.

"*You* knew," Pat said, his eyes flashing at Jane. "You knew she was married and didn't warn me...."

"My dear Pat," she said coldly. "I don't give away other people's secrets. It was not my place to warn you, neither was it my story to tell."

He flushed a dark crimson.

"Perhaps not. And you would be loyal. It's just as well there is some loyalty left in the world."

Sonia put the back of her hand against her mouth and looked at him piteously.

"Pat, how can you be so hard?"

"Do you blame me? Can't you see what you've done to me? You should have told me the truth long ago. It's you who have been hard—and cruel."

Jane, her heart pounding, hurting, measured *his* hurt, his broken faith, his wounded pride, and could have wept for him. But she felt there was nothing for her to do but to go out and leave these two alone.

She went up to her bedroom. She did not switch on the light, but stood a moment by the window. She could see nothing but Pat's face, white, hurt, bitterly angry. She suffered for and with him. She would have given much to spare him this knowledge and this pain. Yet she could do nothing. All her love for him was useless. She could not even comfort him. It was the realisation that her love was so futile that defeated Jane to-night. When she turned away from the window, the tears were pouring down her cheeks.

In the deserted Moorish Court, Sonia and Pat talked together. But not for long. Feeling was too high on both sides and although Sonia, womanlike, half enjoyed a big dramatic scene, Pat wanted to fly from it.

He would have left her when Jane did, but she caught

his hand, and implored him hysterically to stay and listen to her.

"What is there to be said?" he asked her roughly. "Unless you want to give me all the lurid details of your marriage with this Frenchman."

"He isn't altogether French—he's half-English."

"All the same to me if he's Portuguese."

Sonia stopped crying. She gave Pat a resentful look from under long wet lashes.

"I thought you loved me . . . if you did, you couldn't be so brutal. . . ."

He stared at her incredulously.

"Brutal! I? And how about you? Could anything have been more brutal than your treatment of me? I believed in you. I loved you so much that I would have staked my life on you. And I would have lost it. Well, I *have* lost all that really counted."

"It's just as hard on me."

"I deny that. You haven't suddenly discovered *my* wife, in my arms."

"I never wanted to be in Maurice's arms. It's the last thing I wanted."

He gave her another incredulous look.

"I just don't understand you, Sonia. How could you have imagined that you'd keep me by leading me on with all sorts of hopes you knew must inevitably be wrecked? I presume the Chief doesn't know either."

"No," she whispered. "Nobody does—except Jane."

The story poured out then. As far as Pat could tell, he was hearing the truth now, when he learned of the foolish infatuation which had led Sonia into the crazy marriage with Maurice Gardener in Paris, two years ago. She excused herself on every score. She had been young, impressionable, spoiled, she said. And he was ready to believe her and to credit that the whole thing had been a mad mistake which many another lovely, foolish girl might have made.

But there seemed to him nothing to excuse her cowardice in keeping the story from him. Even if she had, justifiably, been too frightened to confess to her father, she should never have withheld facts from him, Pat. For he had truly loved her, and true love, surely, deserves fair and courageous treatment.

"You let me think that I was going to marry you—work for you—and it wasn't true. You just made a fool of me!" he reproached her bitterly.

"But I wanted to marry you. Pat, don't you love me enough even now to wait until I can get a divorce?"

He was silent a moment. He had been so shocked by the discovery that Sonia was married that his brain had scarcely had time to smooth things out, or analyse his emotions. But as he looked down at her, his beloved one, who was fair as a lily, beautiful as a poem, his heart gave a great jerk of red-hot pain. He had loved her so very much. Too much! The goddess had tumbled from her pedestal and lay shattered at his feet. How could he ever feel the same about her again?

She caught his arm and looked up at him with swimming eyes.

"Pat, Pat, don't be too hard on me. . . ."

He found himself shaking.

"You don't understand what this has done to me, Sonia. I absolutely counted on you and your love?"

"But I do love you . . . I swear it."

"Do you? How much? So much that you'd come with me this very moment to your father and tell him the truth? So much that you'd tell him everything that you've told me and then go away with me and let Gardener divorce you, and start life with me somewhere? Would you do that? Would you, Sonia?"

For an instant she stared at him wildly. Then her lashes drooped, her cheeks scorched.

"Daddy would chuck me straight out and you too, and we wouldn't have a cent...."

"Ah! You're being cautious. The financial side comes into it, does it? It wouldn't appeal to you to take my hand and wander with me like a gypsy, away over the hills? That would be too sentimental, too romantic. You'd rather have the Victor to drive you to the stars, eh?"

She snatched her hand away.

"Now you're being melodramatic and hateful."

"No, I'm being honest with myself and trying to make you honest, too. But you don't love me enough to be chucked out with me, do you? You want a watertight position before you tell your father anything about your husband—or your lover!"

She flared into temper like a spoiled child.

"Pat, you're just being a fool! Don't you see that if we handle things carefully we can still have a wonderful time, and there wouldn't be any need to face poverty or disgrace?"

Silence between them. In that instant the last shred of faith in her seemed to be torn from his heart by the very roots. He felt sick with disappointment. Then she made the final mistake. She came close to him, put her arms about his neck and strove by sheer physical allure to win back his admiration.

For a fraction of a minute all his senses stirred in response. His arms went round her savagely. He had never been more in love with any woman in his life than with this one, never wanted anything as madly as possession of her—complete possession.

Then he saw something unbeautiful, distorted in her mind which blotted out the beauty of her face and form. She loved him, but not enough to make a sacrifice for him. That wasn't love as he understood it. That wasn't what he was going to accept, no matter how attractive it seemed on the surface.

Speechlessly he thrust her away from him, turned and rushed away, out of her sight.

CHAPTER FOURTEEN

JANE went in search of Sonia.

Jane had had her "cry" and finished with it. Now, anxious for her cousin, she went through the hotel to look for her. She found her still sitting there in the Moorish court.

"Hadn't you better go to bed?" Jane said kindly. "It's been a horrible evening for all of us, and it's no good talking about it now. We must wait and see what happens in the morning. You've got Maurice to deal with. I presume you still don't intend to tell Uncle John."

"I do not. I've had enough for the time being," said Sonia bitterly. "I'm more than ever determined not to tell Daddy."

Jane said nothing. She felt that it was hopeless to try to argue with Sonia. Glancing at her wristwatch, she saw that it was nearly eleven. Where was Pat? She felt ill-at-ease and miserable at the memory of his stricken face. She said:

"Where did Pat go?"

"I don't know," said Sonia, and began to cry again.

Jane took her firmly to her bedroom and left her there. She could see perfectly well that Sonia was not going to tackle any of the problems with either courage or sense. She must just remain what she was—a supreme egotist.

She, Jane, would have to see Maurice in the morning. She would have to talk to him and try to induce him to let Sonia alone, or arrange a quiet divorce.

Meanwhile she found it impossible to go to bed until she had made sure that Pat was all right. She knew that he had been hit hard by to-night's revelation and that it might go badly with one of his hot Irish temperament.

With her Spanish shawl around her shoulders, Jane searched El Minza for Pat. But Pat was nowhere to be found. She telephoned to the servants' quarters and was told that Mr. Royale's chauffeur was not in his room.

After that Jane began to be afraid. Where *was* Pat? What had he done when he had left Sonia? How far had he been affected by the discovery of the truth about her? Perhaps it had just driven him wild, and he was in the mood not to care what he did.

A dozen alarming conjectures shaped themselves in Jane's mind. And the knowledge came to her that she had really never loved until to-night. But to-night she loved Pat Connel with all that was fierce and passionate and, simultaneously, protective and maternal in her. She was conscious of nothing but the overwhelming desire to help him, and if necessary, save him from himself.

She knew that she must find him before she closed her eyes in sleep to-night.

The hotel guide, a brown-skinned, dark-eyed Algerian with a red fez at an insolent angle on his sleek black head, was lounging on the entrance steps, arms folded, a cigarette between his lips.

Jane addressed him. Immediately the figure in the luminous white robes leaped to attention.

"Lady?"

She asked him if he had seen a young Englishman in a grey flannel suit . . . blue eyes, black hair . . . he was wearing a green chauffeur's uniform when he arrived at the hotel this afternoon.

The guide gave Jane a flashing smile.

Yes, he had seen the gentleman. In fact, half an hour ago he had been in conversation with him. The gentleman had wanted distraction and had asked where he might find gaiety and music in the town.

"Where did you send him?" she asked the guide.

"To Lotus Café, lady. Very gay there! Moorish girls dancing . . . Moorish music . . . best in Morocco."

Jane stared in front of her. It did not take her long to make up her mind what she was going to do. She said promptly:

"Take me there."

The guide stared. His eyes expressed horror.

"Lotus Café not for lady. Only for gentleman."

Jane's lips tightened.

"You can look after me. I wish to go there."

The guide salaamed.

"If lady pleases . . . shall I order conveyance?"

"How far is it?"

"Way down hill. Near main street."

"Then get the hotel car."

The guide hastened to do her bidding. He saw money in it and that was all that mattered to him. If the pretty little English lady, who held her shawl firmly about her as though to hide her charms rather than flaunt them in the manner of his own women, wished to go to the infamous café, she must do so. After all he was used to receiving queer orders . . . particularly from American ladies, who found these places of entertainment "all too cute".

The car drew up outside a narrow white house with green shutters. From the lower windows came an orange glow of light, and a noise which seemed to Jane to have a close association with the wailing of cats on the roof tops. It was the shrill incantation to the accompaniment of pipes, known as Moorish music.

The guide helped Jane out of the car.

"Lotus Café, lady."

"Wait for me here one moment," she said.

She pushed aside the striped curtain and looked into the room. For a moment she saw nothing clearly. The café was veiled in a thick haze of smoke. It was unbearably hot.

Then Jane's blinking eyes focused upon three half-naked girls with brown glistening bodies performing some kind of slow dance in the centre of the floor. Around them, at little tables, sat a motley crowd. Mostly Arabs with white or striped burnous, Algerians with the red fez, Spanish uniformed police, and one or two English or American men.

Jane quailed at the idea of entering. It was only her violent desire to save Pat that kept her standing there at all, because she had an instinctive desire to hide herself from the bold gazes that were directed at her once her presence was noticed in the doorway.

Then her heart gave a great leap. She saw the man for whom she was searching. Pat was sitting alone at one of the tables, a glass in his hand. Quite plainly now she saw his face. It looked very white, glistening as though with sweat in the garish light. A profoundly tragic face, all the humour and boyishness wiped from it. He stared without any particular interest at the undulating figures of the Moorish girls.

And this was the gaiety which he was seeking, this the oblivion from that searing pain of having loved somebody who wasn't worthy. . . .

Suddenly Jane called his name, loudly and clearly, so that her voice carried above the wailing chant of the native musician.

"Pat!"

His head shot up. He looked in her direction. With immense astonishment he recognised that small figure in the light camels'-hair coat, belted round the waist, small hands thrust in the pockets.

"Jane," he said stupidly.

She beckoned to him. He rose to his feet. He was a little drunk, but not very. He paid his bill, quite aware that he was being charged three times more than the drinks were worth and in no mood to dispute it. He came straight through the smoke-thickened café, took Jane's arm, led her outside, and let the striped curtain fall behind them.

"What the hell are you doing here?" he asked.

His voice was like his eyes, rather blurred. But Jane looked at him with profound relief, a relief so great that she could have wept. If nothing more than this had happened to him—she need not have worried her head off about him.

"You idiot, Pat Connel!" she said in a furious little voice. "You prize idiot!"

"Why, may I ask?"

"Coming down to a place like this and getting tight."

"I'm not tight."

"Not very," she admitted. "But if you'd sat there much longer you'd have been *very* . . . then anything might have happened to you in that thieving, pock-marked crowd."

He dropped her arm, pulled a cigarette from his pocket and lit it. As he flung away the burnt match he stared down at her flushed angry young face.

"Who told you I was here?"

"I asked the hotel guide."

"How indiscreet of him!" said Pat, and laughed, but the laugh was not a blithe sound.

"Perhaps it was indiscreet of me to come and look for you, but I'm glad I did."

"What did you suppose was going to happen to me?"

Her lashes drooped. She felt suddenly embarrassed.

"Oh, I don't know. I daresay I've been a fool. . . ."

His mind, which had been fogged by the fumes of bad alcohol, began to clear. Out here where it was fresh, cool, crystal clear in the spring moonlight, he could breath again, think again. He didn't want to think. He had gone there into that rotten stupefying place of amusement for the express purpose of being stupefied. That was what he wanted . . . something that would stop him remembering Sonia and what she had done to him.

"You should have left me alone," he said.

Jane's breath came more quickly. With all her heart she longed to put an arm about him and tell him not to suffer like this about Sonia, to assure him that it wasn't worth it. But she could do nothing but feel hurt and foolish because she had made a blunder in following him.

"I know I had no right to interfere," she said. "I don't know what made me come. I'll go back."

She turned to the car and the guide opened the door for her. Pat followed.

"I might as well come too."

"Do as you wish," she said coldly. "But I don't advise you to swallow any more of that synthetic whisky. It will make you feel awful in the morning."

He gave a brief laugh, and swung himself into the car beside her.

"Dear little Jane, I've never known you not to have a sensible word ready for an emergency. And you're always right. That's the worst of it. You've been right all the way along. Only I haven't believed you. I didn't want to . . . oh, *hell!*"

He suddenly sat back in the corner of the car and put the back of his hand across his eyes.

The guide discreetly slammed the door.

"I walk back, lady."

The car moved on. Jane sat still, conscious of little satisfaction because she had "always been right".

Pat said:

"You were darned right about that whisky. God, it was foul! The whole café was foul."

"Yes," said Jane.

"I felt crazy. I wanted to get tight. I was for a bit, but I'm not now. I see it's no use. Good old Dowson knew all about it. 'I called for madder music, stronger wine, hoping to put thy pale lost lilies out of sight . . .'"

"Please," interrupted Jane. "Don't quote *Cynara* to me."

"No, it's cheap, isn't it? I feel a bit cheap."

Her love and pity for him battled with the desire to be intensely angry with him. Impulsively she put out her hand. He clung to the small cool fingers as a drowning man clutches at a straw.

"I'm not cross, really," said Jane. "I'm dreadfully grieved for you."

"Sure and I've been a double-dyed ass," he said, his rich Irish voice breaking suddenly. "But I loved her so much, Jane. I adored her!"

"I know."

"She shouldn't have let me go on believing I had a right to her love."

"She's a queer girl, Pat. She's been so spoiled all her life, I suppose one must try to make excuses if she isn't as rational as other people."

"You can excuse her. I can't. I shall never forgive her for not telling me that she was married."

"It's been a frightful position for me. I wanted to warn you. I couldn't."

"You've been mighty loyal to her."

"You wouldn't have expected me to betray her."

He looked down at the small firm little hand which he was holding, and then up at Jane. Her face was pale and tender in the moonlight. And her eyes were very sad. He had been struck once or twice by the sadness in Jane's eyes. He was conscious of a great warmth of admiration and respect and liking for her.

"I wouldn't expect *you* to betray anybody," he said. "Although at one time to-night I felt I had no faith left in anyone."

She thrilled to his praise.

"You must keep faith with yourself, Pat—that's all that matters."

"Why do you bother about me? Why have you ever bothered about me?"

She sat very still, scarcely daring to breathe. This was where she must guard her secret very well indeed. At length she said:

"I suppose it's because I like you—because I've always liked you."

He looked down at her. She was looking straight up at him. Her eyes seemed very clear and bright and beautiful. Even in the midst of his misery, his furious resentment against Sonia, the lies which had smashed his faith and his ideals, he was still man enough to be conscious of Jane Daunt's attractions. He put an arm about her shoulder, drew her to his side and said:

"Thank you, Jane. Thank you, my dear."

Her eyes suddenly closed in a frightened way. She sat very still, not daring to move. She felt both bitterness and rapture in the circle of his arm. His head was resting against her shoulder in a weary dejected way. He was rather like a tired, dispirited little boy. There was no question of sex in that embrace. Her own blood might be leaping wildly because of his proximity, but she knew that there was no passion in him—only a craving for comfort, for sanctuary, somebody to help him bear the intense pain of his disillusionment.

All that was proud and reserved in Jane made her want to push him away, to cry out sharply:

"Don't! Don't touch me. I'm not here ready for the asking, just because Sonia has failed you!"

But there was something deeper, warmer, and much more human than that which made her oblivious of her own feelings to-night. She was concentrating on him. She put both arms around him and said:

"Poor dear! Poor dear Pat!"

Neither of them spoke again. But they sat like that with their arms clasped about each other, while the hotel car climbed the steep hill towards El Minza.

During those few moments Jane was absurdly, wildly happy. And he was absurdly, wildly unhappy. But the comfort and security of their embrace seemed to draw the sting out of things, or at least made them more bearable for him.

Just before they reached the hotel, they drew apart again, but he kept hold of her hands.

"I can't pretend to thank you," he said huskily. "I don't suppose I shall ever be able to tell you how much you've done for me to-night."

Now that his arms were no longer around her she was filled with sudden embarrassment. A hot blush enveloped her whole body.

"There's nothing to thank me for, Pat," she said; but did not look at him.

"Plenty," he said. "To begin with, I expect you saved me from making a complete fool of myself."

She tried to laugh.

"Glad I was of some use, Pat. I know how badly you feel. But don't let it sink you. You're much too good a fellow for that. And don't let Sonia have the satisfaction of thinking she can break you."

With a quick nervous gesture, Pat smoothed his hair back from his forehead, then took a packet of cigarettes from his pocket. He offered Jane one but she refused. He lit one for himself. As he put it between his lips, he said:

"Believe me, I'm not interested in what Sonia thinks."

"That may or may not be true," said Jane. "You feel that way to-night, but—"

He turned on her.

"Do you think I could ever forget—"

She interrupted:

"I don't say that at all. But naturally you're feeling raw to-night."

"And I shall feel raw to-morrow," he said. "And the next day and the next."

Jane felt unutterably tender toward him. Poor hurt Pat! Funny how like a small hurt boy he seemed to her to-night.

She said:

"It'll get better, Pat. These things do, you know."

He shrugged his shoulders. The car was drawing up outside the hotel entrance. Pat stepped out, helped Jane, then paid the man.

The car moved away, and left them standing there on the hotel steps. The moonlight was still flooding Tangier with that bright unearthly splendour. It was growing colder. Jane shivered as she looked at her watch.

"It's late," she said. "I think we'd both better go to bed, don't you?"

"You ought to have been in bed long ago," he said. "I

feel frightfully guilty about it . . . I had no idea you'd worry about me . . . for me . . . it as sweet of you, Jane!"

She turned away and began moving to the hotel.

"See you in the morning, Pat. Try and sleep now, won't you?"

"Wait a moment," he said.

She turned back and smiled. "Yes?"

"I'm not going on with this trip."

She looked him straight in the eyes.

"Yes, you are, Pat," she said.

"I'm not! Do you think I could stand hours and days of this journey with *her* . . . never getting away from her . . . after all that's happened . . . it would be a bit too much!"

"Pat," said Jane quietly, "I've always thought Sonia an egotist—and—I think you're one, too."

"What is egotistical in it?"

"You are concentrating on yourself and your own reactions. But I think you have my uncle to consider, too. In that rather mad fashion of yours, you took Woodham's place. You volunteered to be our chauffeur. Then you got yourself into a row, and upset everything and everybody, after which Uncle John forgave you and took you back. Now you're going to walk out on him. You know that he's been looking forward to driving over the mountains more than anything. You don't hesitate to land him in difficulties, do you? He won't tolerate strange drivers. He's depending on you; must *he* suffer because of this mess? I admit that most of it is Sonia's fault. But you're a bit to blame too, Pat, for rushing into the affair, aren't you? From the beginning it was bound to be disastrous!"

He had listened to her speech, smoking quickly, his eyes fixed on the luminous distance. Then he said:

"If Sonia had been free to marry me, as I thought she was, it wouldn't have been a disaster."

"Even so, I fail to see why Uncle John should suffer for it!"

Pat bit his lips.

"Yes, you're right about that."

"You say I'm always right, don't you?" she asked, with a sudden humorous smile.

"But, Jane, I don't want to go on! I want to get back to London. I want to forget Sonia. I want to put this thing behind me and start again."

"You can do that when the trip's over, Pat. You won't feel better for letting everybody down, will you?"

"Oh, confound you, Jane Daunt!" he said angrily. "Why the dickens must you always be right?"

"Stick it, Pat!" she said. "Don't go back on us now. Make yourself carry on in spite of what has happened. In spite of Sonia."

"And how do you think she's going to feel about it? What's she going to do? What's that miserable husband of hers going to do?"

"I don't know. He's a nuisance and always has been one."

"Why did she ever marry him—" he began, then he stopped and set his teeth. "No, I don't want to begin thinking about that. It's been circling round and round my head ever since I found out . . . it has driven me mad."

"I think money may settle him," said Jane. "It always has done in the past. Certainly, I want her to tell her father, and get the thing over and done with. I always have wanted her to do that, but she won't. She's afraid."

"I would never have thought her capable—" began Pat, but stopped himself again. It was too awful that love . . . such love as he had felt for Sonia should turn to bitterness . . . to contempt. Once he had felt so unworthy of her love. Horrible now to feel that *she* was unworthy to be loved!

"I daresay there'll be trouble," said Jane. "But I'll see Maurice in the morning and try to make him more reasonable. He gave her away to you to-night. But I think he's too much of a coward to do so to Uncle John. He knows perfectly well that he wouldn't get another penny."

Pat looked at her with horror in his eyes.

Sonia had been sending Maurice Gardener money . . . blackmailed by her own husband. It was beastly, beastly!

"Stop thinking about it, Pat. Go to bed and forget," said Jane.

He pitched his cigarette into the darkness.

"Very well."

She came nearer to him and touched his arm.

"And Pat, be big," she said. "Big enough to help Uncle John. I know it won't be easy if you have to see Sonia every day. But you can do anything if you make up your mind to it."

"I believe you could, Jane Daunt!" he said.

"You, too."

"Oh, very well, since you've decided everything for me, I'll try not to walk out."

"I don't want to make your decisions for you, Pat. It's nothing to do with me really. But I'm your friend . . ." her voice choked a little on that word ". . . As a friend, I ask you to stay and see the trip through."

"I will, Jane," he said. "Good night, my dear. Good night, and thank you again."

She held out her hand. He took it and raised it to his lips. It was a gesture of homage and gratitude. But it shook Jane's nerve. She longed to cry out:

"Oh Pat, Pat, I love you so! So desperately! Pat, don't let the thought of Sonia hurt you any more. Let me love you . . . *let me!*"

But she did nothing of the sort. She drew her hand away, turned, and walked into the hotel.

CHAPTER FIFTEEN

JANE awakened that next morning to find Sonia standing by her bedside, and the sunlight streaming brilliantly into the room. She sat up and rubbed her eyes.

"Hullo! Is it very late?"

"No, it's quite early," said Sonia. "But I had to come and talk to you. Look."

She held out a sheet of notepaper, scribbled over in a slanting untidy hand.

"From Maurice. Pushed under my door."

Jane pushed her dark tumbled hair out of her eyes and, hunching her knees, took the note that Sonia handed her. She yawned.

"Gosh! I'm tired!"

"Haven't you slept? I haven't! Not a wink!"

"I slept like a horse, but I was pretty late getting to bed?"

"Where were you last night?" asked Sonia, regarding Jane curiously. "I felt frightfully worried and miserable after I got to bed so I came along to talk to you, but you weren't here."

"No," said Jane, without meeting her cousin's gaze. "I was out."

"Out! Who with? What were you doing out at that time of night?"

"I was with Pat," said Jane abruptly.

"With Pat, were you? And what had he to say to you?"

"Quite a lot," answered Jane.

"Aren't you going to tell me?"

"Let me read this letter first of all."

"Well, that solves one difficulty anyhow," said Sonia. "In fact it solves quite a good many. Maurice has gone. He left after an early breakfast."

"We're leaving too."

"But he didn't know that. He just thought he'd be doing me a good turn by clearing out. I think he was sorry for last night."

Jane was wide awake now. She read what Maurice had written, and with considerable relief. Certainly he was saving them all a lot of trouble.

"Dear Sonia,

"On thinking things over I have decided that I behaved like a cad to-night. I had no right to break my word and give you away. I suppose I was a cad ever to marry you. I see it is useless trying to effect any sort of reconciliation between us since you're in love with this other fellow and you don't want me. I only hope I haven't upset your apple-cart too badly. Anyhow, I'm not going to make trouble between you and your father. I'll clear out of the hotel and disappear. Don't worry about me any more.

"I hate to mention money but things are rather bad with me and so if you can send me a little now and again, do so for old time's sake, *cherie*.

"I think it's more than possible that I may give you grounds for divorce in the near future. You may communicate with me at my old address in Paris.

         "Yours,

              "Maurice."

Jane looked up at her cousin.

"Well, that's the best thing he's ever done."

"Having done the worst last night," said Sonia bitterly.

"He came between me and Pat. That's all that really matters to me."

Jane reached for a cigarette, lit it, picked up the telephone and ordered a cup of tea, then lay back on her pillow and smoked thoughtfully.

"Thank God, there won't have to be a scene or argument with Maurice. He's come to his senses at last. I think it scared him . . . being knocked down by Pat in that way. Of course he knows perfectly well, too, if he gave you away to Uncle John, he'd never get another shilling. It's money that really counts with Maurice."

Sonia got up and began to pace the room restlessly. She looked haggard and wretched. The sleepless nights had marred her loveliness. She said:

"Maurice may be out of the way, and it may even look as though he'll give me a divorce. That would be pretty wonderful, but I've lost Pat. I have lost him, haven't I?" She turned and faced Jane. "I suppose you know all there is to know. He talked to you, didn't he? Go on, Jane. Tell me what he said. Tell me. I've got a right to know."

"Sonia," said Jane, "I'm not going to tell you anything about last night except that Pat very nearly made a fool of himself because he was so unhappy about you, and I stepped in and stopped him. That's all. It's been a ghastly shock to him and you can't be surprised. You can take it for granted things are over between you two."

"Why should they be?" Sonia suddenly flashed, cheeks crimson, eyes blazing. "Why should they if I can get my freedom? If Pat really loves me, he'll forgive me. You can't wipe out love all in a minute like that."

"Oh yes you can!" said Jane grimly. "And I think you wiped it out last night very thoroughly."

Sonia drew near the bed, her small hands clenched to her sides.

"Has he told you that he'll never forgive me?"

"Yes," said Jane quietly.

"I don't see why he shouldn't."

"You may have no pride, Sonia. He has plenty, and in spite of this hole-in-the-corner affair with you, he has a sense of honour and straightness. He never could forgive you for leading him on and encouraging him to love you when you knew the position you were in."

Sonia raised her head, a handkerchief to her quivering lips.

"And are we all continuing the trip in this atmosphere?" she demanded. "It'll be charming, won't it? So friendly, so smooth!" she ended, with an hysterical laugh.

"As far as I know we're continuing," Jane said. "You've considered yourself since this holiday began. Now you must think of Uncle John. He's frightfully keen on it all and he's enjoying the rest, looking forward to writing his book. We needn't all get dramatic and break up the party and worry him to death, need we?"

"I suppose not."

"I daresay it won't be pleasant. But you'll just have to make the best of it."

"With Pat and myself not on speaking terms, eh?" said Sonia. "That will be fun!"

"You've had your fun."

"Oh, how cruel you are!" said Sonia, breaking into fresh sobbing.

"I don't mean to be cruel," said Jane. "But you would have this affair, now you must put up with the results. It will be just as unpleasant for Pat. Only for God's sake *leave him alone.*"

Sonia did not reply. She sat with hunched-up shoulders in an attitude that suggested defiance. Her thoughts ran on indiscriminately. In her fashion she was still in love with Pat. The very fact that she had lost him made her want him more. She was not going to give him up without a struggle. She foresaw that if they did all go on with this journey across the Riff mountains, she would be in daily contact with Pat. Well, he had loved her madly. She was not prepared to believe that all that feeling was dead and gone.

She still had her youth and beauty and brilliance. He could not be blind to it all. Surely, in time, he would fall under the spell of her charm once more. He would forgive her. They could begin again. And this time she would be free. Maurice was going to set her free.

The tears dried on Sonia's lashes then. Hope sprang anew in her heart. She was undefeated. And as usual she was thinking of nobody's point of view save her own.

She rose from the bed and stretched herself.

"Oh, well, I suppose we'd better get dressed. Daddy will want to get on. Thank God, Maurice has gone. That's lifted a weight off my shoulders. Now we're going into the wilderness, aren't we? I believe these mountains are terribly lonely and primitive."

"Terribly," echoed Jane.

Sonia went out. Jane lay still after she had gone. She, too, was thinking. Sonia's swift change from despair to cheerfulness worried her not a little. She knew her cousin so well. She half guessed what lay at the back of her mind. Sonia meant to try to win Pat back again. Well, did that matter to her, Jane? It never entered her head to try to win Pat on the rebound. She wasn't made that way. On the other hand, she did think of him. Would it be for his happiness, his ultimate good, if he succumbed to Sonia's charms again?

The memory of the deception Sonia had practised upon him and all the lies she had told, could never wholly be wiped out. He would never love her again in the same idealistic, whole-hearted fashion. It was Jane's belief that he would never love Sonia again at all. In any case, the prospect of watching Sonia make a fight for him, of Pat being hurt all over again, did not appeal to Jane.

She got up, put on her dressing-gown, and went along to the bathroom in a mood of depression. She thought with a wry smile how lucky her uncle was. He was the only person who looked forward to this journey with any real pleasure, blissfully ignorant as he was of all the trouble going on around him. Dear old Uncle John!

At ten o'clock Mr. Royale emerged from the hotel ready for the day's journey. The Victor was there, sleek and shining for them, with Pat at the wheel. Jane and Sonia followed Mr. Royale to the car. Pat gave them all a cold, detached look, touched his cap and said:

"Good morning!"

For the fraction of an instant Pat's gaze rested upon the figure of Sonia. Beautiful and desirable as ever. But this morning, desire seemed cold in Pat's heart. He was conscious only of bitterness. With icy politeness he touched his cap, said "Good morning," and set about helping with the luggage.

Mr. Royale—no longer worried by the thought that there was a "flirtation" going on between his daughter and young Connel—all that nonsense, he imagined, had been left behind them—seated himself in the back of his car with his niece, who was to take notes of their travels.

Sonia took her accustomed seat beside the driver. She stole a look at him. She had taken special pains with her toilet this morning. She had touched up eyes and cheeks, removed the traces of her sleepless night, and put on a new and attractive suit of almond green, with a thin Hungarian blouse exquisitely embroidered.

But Pat did not turn his head to look at her. He drove away from El Minza with a stony face, his gaze fixed on the road before him. He was conscious only of that fierce resentment against Sonia. He almost hated her because of her grace, her beauty, all that had ever fired his imagination, all that had made a fool of him. The familiar, intoxicating perfume which emanated from her was an irritation now rather than a stimulant.

Jane, taking shorthand notes at her uncle's dictation, glanced up now and then at the two in front of her. She could hear Sonia making an attempt at conversation, which was responded to by Pat only with cold formality. Not once did he look at her. Little doubt Sonia must feel chagrined and thwarted. But it was Pat whom Jane pitied. She knew of those two it was Pat who really suffered.

Jane found it hard to concentrate on her work. Several times she had to interrupt her uncle and ask what he had said.

"What's the matter with you, my dear?" he said, surprised by her unusual inaccuracy.

She had no excuse to offer. She only knew that she found it hard to concentrate. She kept thinking about last night—last night when the hotel car had driven Pat and herself back to El Minza, and they had clung close to each other. He, blind with pain and misery, seeking desperately for comfort. She, only too ready to give it, loving him with all her soul. This love business wasn't fair, Jane cried to herself. *It wasn't fair.* It hurt far too much.

Pat went on answering Sonia's artless questions abruptly—almost rudely. He would have given anything to find that it was all a nightmare; to wake up, be able to look into Sonia's large shining eyes and know that she spoke the truth, and had always spoken the truth, know that she loved him and he could rely upon her love; that one day he would make her his wife.

There were grim difficulties ahead of him. He knew that well enough. As soon as they got back to London he must leave John Royale's service. He would not stay in the

Victor Company, nor see anybody that reminded him of Sonia. Life stretched before him a blank—just a blank—nothing more.

They left Tangier behind them. The white minarets, the mosaic mosque, faded into a blue distance. They were on the dusty, winding road which led to the mountains—those sinister ranges where there had been so much fighting amongst the Riffs.

Sonia looked about her gloomily. She did not care much for the aspect of those dark remote peaks and this rough territory. She was miserable. The savage country made her more miserable.

But it appealed to Jane. This was real Morocco. It had a fierce, proud beauty of its own. It appealed to all that was remote and proud in her.

It did not seem long before they were swallowed up in the dark valleys between the mountains. The road grew more lonely; the surface stony and the ground on either side of them was a greenish brown, dotted with stunted palms and shrubs. In the distance, through a mist of blue, the mountain peaks were veiled in low-lying rain clouds. But above them the heavens were clear and the sunshine brilliant.

It looked as though at any moment they might plunge into a storm of rain. The big black storm clouds rolling up on the horizon were grand and awe-inspiring.

Everywhere grew the little purple ground irises, fields of them, the spring flowers of Morocco.

Now and then they passed a solitary Arab on foot, or riding a donkey. Sometimes women padded along on bare feet, wearing shawls and striped petticoats, and these unveiled women of the hills inspired John Royale to make copious notes. It was all amazingly like a scene from ancient Jerusalem, he announced.

But Sonia was not interested. She turned round to her father and said:

"Where are we getting to? It's horribly lonely. I'm sure we'll be attacked and robbed."

"I doubt that, my dear," said Mr. Royale. "Mind you, there was a case of kidnapping not so very long ago—an English newspaper correspondent was carried off and held for ransom. But I don't see why we should be. We're not important enough."

Sonia glanced at Pat.

"I might be carried off and sold in a slave market," she said childishly.

Pat's face did not move a muscle. But he was thinking:

"Yes, that's what you would deserve. To be sold as a slave . . . to be whipped . . . to be made to suffer as you make men suffer. . . ."

When they had been driving a couple of hours, they stopped for a breathing space and had the drinks and sandwiches from the lunch basket which they had brought from El Minza.

Mr. Royale and Pat examined the map between them. They had left the main road which leads from Tangier to Ceuta. They had taken a less sophisticated route which Mr. Royale chose because it would eventually land them at Pogador—a Moorish town in the valley said to contain relics of architecture dating back from thousands of years B.C.

"We should reach Pogador before dark, shouldn't we?" inquired Mr. Royale.

Pat nodded. "Yes, sir."

"What sort of place is Pogador?" queried Sonia pettishly. "Sounds awful to me."

"Aren't you enjoying it, Babe?" asked her father.

"No," she said abruptly.

"But you've been in such high spirits all the way along,"

he said, and eyed her a trifle anxiously. "Feeling quite fit, aren't you, darling?"

"Quite, thanks, Daddy."

Mr. Royale turned to his niece.

"What's wrong with her, Jane?"

"Oh, just a little bored with it, perhaps," said Jane, hedging.

But Sonia looked at Pat and this time Pat looked straight back at her. Into her large limpid eyes came a look of pleading. But his were dark and bitter. She took a sudden step towards him.

"Pat," she whispered under her breath.

"Can I do anything for you, miss?" he asked in a cold, deliberate voice.

She turned away, scarlet and furious.

When they moved on Mr. Royale suggested that his daughter should sit beside him.

"Come and hold your old Daddy's hand, Babe," he said affectionately, "and let Jane have a rest from work."

Sonia had no other choice but to fall in with his suggestion. But looking at the back of Pat's handsome head, she swore to herself that she would make him change his feelings before this journey ended. He should not look at her like that, coldly, dispassionately. He *should* not.

Jane, seated beside Pat, maintained a silence which he eventually broke.

"Jolly little journey, isn't it?"

"It's such a pity," said Jane, "that we have to concentrate upon our personal emotions. There's so much to be got out of everything else. Look at the grandeur of this scenery. Don't the mountains make you feel that all our dramas are petty and futile?"

Pat's set face relaxed a little.

"Not so much petty as futile, Jane. Love, hatred, all the emotions are *quite* futile!"

She winced.

"As I told you last night, my dear, you mustn't let it hurt you too badly."

"Ah, but you don't know what it is to love, Jane."

She was on the point of denying that violently and saying to him:

"It isn't true! I *do* know what it is to love . . . suffer . . . to watch the man I love being hurt by another woman! Isn't that bad enough?"

But she said nothing. After the pause Pat added:

"How completely circumstances can alter one's outlook! This time yesterday I was glad to be alive, there was so much to look forward to. To-day, I don't really feel I'd care if we were set upon by a lot of cut-throats and finished off."

Jane smiled grimly.

"Speak for yourself, Mr. Connel. I don't want my throat slit, thank you."

"It's much too nice a throat to slit, anyhow," he said, with a flash of his old gallantry.

Jane actually blushed.

"Idiot!" she said.

Suddenly he felt the warmth of her friendship flowing to him. It pulled him out of the darkness, the almost suicidal mood in which he had set forth from Tangier. She was great, this Jane, she was fine and strong. Any fellow on earth would feel glad of her friendship.

CHAPTER SIXTEEN

THEY came to Pogador after what seemed an interminable run of two hundred miles across the mountains. Sonia was depressed and bad tempered and did not join in the general enthusiasm as they drove down a steep hill and sighted the lovely old town.

The big Victor purred slowly and smoothly through narrow streets that were cobbled and indescribably filthy; nevertheless the white walls, the blue arches, the old Eastern houses crowding one upon the other crazily, with little space for air, presented a picture of purest beauty.

Across heavily latticed, barred windows, climbed masses of flowering creeper. Gardens were gay with cerise geraniums, and the delicate pink of almond blossom now in full bloom.

"Oh, it's marvellous!" cried Jane, looking to the right and left of her.

"I don't suppose you'll ever see anything more really Moorish than Pogador," said Pat. "I've been here once before. The hotel is only barely fit for tourists, and that's about all I can say, but I think the Chief will get enough copy here."

Mr. Royale was already in raptures. Sonia said nothing. She was nursing a grievance against Jane. Jane could make Pat speak to her. Why should he smile and talk to her like that? Sonia hated Pogador. She complained of the unsavoury odours. She refused to see the fairy-tale fascination of the place.

Pat had to drive very slowly. On either side of the car flowed continual streams of humanity and animals. Donkeys, goats, swarms of half-naked children with enormous black eyes and lovely mischievous faces.

The big English car was regarded with great curiosity. Not many tourists came to Pogador. It was too far out of the usual route. Swarms of little Arab boys rushed after them screaming for *backsheesh*.

Pat guided them at last into a kind of square which was cleaner and more civilised. And here they found their hotel, and it was with some relief that they disembarked from the car and stretched cramped limbs after the long drive.

There was no question in Pogador of chauffeur's quarters. Pat was given a room with the rest of them. And Mr. Royale, in cheerful mood, invited him to dine with the party.

"You brought us here splendidly, Connel. We'll drop the chauffeur business this evening, shall we? Join us for the evening meal."

Pat wanted to refuse. He had not the slightest desire to see so much of Sonia. He tried to escape, but Mr. Royale would have none of it.

"Get out of your uniform, my boy, and then come along and have food with us," he said in his genial fashion.

Pat had no other course but to accept. An invitation from the Chief was, after all, as good as a command.

Sonia cheered up. Pat was going to spend the evening with them in a friendly way and there might be a chance for her to see him alone. She would only have to be alone with him for a few moments. They would talk, and then she would soon make him understand how much she loved him and how sorry she was for what she had done. He *must* be made to look at her again as though he loved her. All day long she had missed that look in Pat's eyes. She was hungry for it.

Jane regarded the evening with some misgivings. She knew perfectly well what lay at the back of her cousin's mind. And she knew, too, that Pat was still feeling raw and bitter and not likely to enjoy his dinner.

The bedrooms were primitive but clean. There was plenty of hot bath water. Presently, refreshed and changed, the little party foregathered in the dining-room for the evening meal.

Sonia appeared somewhat over-dressed for the occasion in evening toilette, black chiffon, which always suited her

145

fair slender beauty, and with a small Spanish mantilla draped over her head. Through the black lace her golden hair gleamed charmingly, and in that dark delicate frame her face looked a little pale and sad. It gave her a haunting look.

"You're like a Goya picture, my dear," her father remarked gallantly.

Sonia glanced through her long lashes at Pat, who had put on a grey lounge suit and just joined the party. He did not return her gaze.

Jane, watching, wondered grimly how this evening would end. The mantilla, the tragic air, the black dress showing the warm white beauty of Sonia's throat and shoulders, were all to attract *him*. Jane knew it. Pat must know it, too. Was this going to be another sleepless night for everybody?

The dinner was poor, the worst they had had on this journey so far. They were the only guests in the hotel. The Algerian waiter who attended them was anxious to please, and they managed to find some sherry which was drinkable. But that was about all.

"I shall be glad to leave Pogador!" said Sonia as they lit their cigarettes. "It's foul!"

"My dear Babe," said her father, "you haven't the right spirit of adventure. If you want the luxury of civilisation you should have remained behind in a place like El Minza. We're going into the wilderness. It will be a wilder and more primitive journey to-morrow, won't it, Connel?" he addressed Pat.

"Much more so, I believe, sir," he said. "Although as a matter of fact I haven't been farther than Pogador myself."

"I think it should be thrilling," said Jane.

"It might be," said Sonia, and looked through her lashes at Pat.

146

They had black coffee—the best part of the meal—in the one and only lounge, which contained a couple of divans piled with striped cushions, white walls hung with Eastern rugs, little inlaid Moorish tables and a jewelled lamp hanging on chains from the ceiling, which gave a rich subdued light.

"It's quite Oriental and romantic, isn't it?" remarked Sonia, with a rather high-pitched laugh.

"Those rugs are worth some money," murmured Mr. Royale. "Jane, my dear, if you've finished your coffee, how about coming along to my room and taking some dictation? I've a good deal to say about this place."

"I'm ready," said Jane.

She caught Pat's gaze as she rose. She had been quiet and nervy all the evening. And Pat was obviously in a state of nerves. It was equally obvious that he did not want to be left alone with Sonia. His eyes half pleaded to Jane to stay. But she had to go. Reluctantly she followed her uncle out of the lounge.

Sonia sat back against one of the cushions on one of the divans. The hour for which she had been waiting had come. Her heart beat fast. Her cheeks were delicately pink. She said:

"Have you a cigarette, Pat?"

Immediately he rose to his feet and offered her his cigarette-case. Courteously he lit a match and applied it to the cigarette for her. But he avoided looking into her eyes. He said in a chilly voice:

"If you'll excuse me, Miss Royale—or should I say *Mrs. Gardener*—I'll get off to bed. I'm rather tired."

Sonia sat bolt upright. Her face scorched with burning colour, her eyes furious.

"How dare you!" she asked under her breath. "Oh, how *dare* you!"

Pat put his heels together and bowed.

"I beg your pardon. *Miss Royale*, if you prefer it."

"You know that I prefer it. You know that nobody else dreams . . ."

"I won't make the mistake again," he cut in.

"It wasn't a mistake. You did it on purpose . . . to hurt me. . . ." she panted.

Pat clenched his hands. He was conscious of strong emotions tearing through his body. And now he looked down at her. He was well aware of the haunting loveliness of that cameo-like face framed by the black lace mantilla. He could feel all the allure of her red amorous lips, her limpid, asking eyes. Yet he was conscious of one outstanding fact. He no longer loved Sonia. He no longer respected her, therefore he no longer loved her. Desire without love . . . that was nothing . . . worse than nothing. He could not enter into it. He could not even be sorry that he had hurt her by using her married name.

"If you don't mind I'll go to my room," he said.

"Is that all you're going to say to me?" she asked in a trembling voice.

"I don't think there's anything else to say."

"There is . . . there are thousands of things."

"Then they're better left unsaid."

She put out a hand and caught at his arm.

"Pat, don't be like this . . . I know I've been rotten to you . . . that I've lied . . . that I was a coward . . . anything that you like . . . only don't be like this. Let's talk it out . . . we can't go on this way . . . after all we've been to each other."

For an instant Pat looked down at her incredulously. Then he said:

"You don't understand. It's because of all we've been to each other that I am through . . . absolutely through, Sonia."

"You mean you don't want to . . . make it up?"

"Make it up!" he echoed. "How can one *make up* a thing like this, Sonia? It isn't just a quarrel . . . a dispute that can be settled."

"But supposing I tell you that I'm going to get my divorce and be free?"

"That doesn't concern me."

"But it does, Pat. It *must*! Oh, surely you haven't lost all your love for me . . . my dear . . . it's all been horrible . . . beastly . . . and I'm to blame, I realise, but there's happiness ahead of us . . . if you'll only try not to be so bitter."

He was stirred by her as he always had been. He knew that she was his for the asking. But when he remembered all that she had done, her cowardice, her dishonesty, those other feelings died in him.

"No, Sonia," he said. "No. There can be no possible happiness ahead of us. We're through. I told you that last night."

"But Pat," she cried. "You can't have stopped loving me altogether. . . ."

"I'm not going to discuss what I feel for you," he said roughly. "I only ask you to leave me alone."

Her face went white. Her eyes looked abnormally large and wild. She was sinking all her pride—ready to stoop to any levels to get him back.

"Then doesn't it mean anything to you that I can get my freedom?"

"It would have done," he said, "if you'd been willing to go away with me last night . . . face poverty and disgrace, anything, as long as we had each other. But I refuse to hang round and just wait till you think that you've got me, plus everything else that you want out of life."

She put the back of her hand against her lips.

"Oh!" she whispered. "You *beast*!"

"I'm sorry," he said, and felt himself shaking.

"I don't believe that you *ever* loved me. . . ."

"You're not capable of judging," he said.

She threw him a speechless look, then rushed out of the room through the striped curtains which led into the hotel entrance. She ran straight into the arms of Jane, who, cigarette between her lips and a fountain-pen in her hand, had come down to find some ink. Sonia knocked the fountain-pen out of her hand, and Jane stooped to pick it up.

Sonia was in a white-hot passion, and as the two girls stood there staring at each other, the last shreds of Sonia's control snapped. She said through her teeth:

"You've done this, *you* . . . !"

"Done what?" demanded Jane, taking the cigarette from her lips.

"You've taken my place with Pat. He believes in you. He likes you. And he just loathes me now. *Loathes* me, I tell you. He hasn't a kind word to say . . . oh, my God, I wish I'd never been born!"

Jane flushed to the roots of her hair. She caught Sonia's arm and shook her a little.

"Be quiet. For heaven's sake, be quiet! . . ."

"You said something to him last night . . . you made things worse, I know you did. . . ."

Jane shook her cousin again. She was quite aware that Sonia was hysterical and not responsible for what she said, but her gaze sped in terror to the striped curtain. If Pat was through there, he would hear every word that Sonia was screaming. Thank goodness nobody else was about. The dimly lit mosaic hall was deserted.

"Sonia, you must be quiet. You know it's not true. I've always tried to help you."

"But you're in love with Pat yourself. You can't deny it. You're glad Maurice ruined things between me and

Pat. You want Pat for yourself . . . you can't deny that you're in love with him. . . ."

Jane was as white now as she had been red. She found herself shaking. She dropped Sonia's arm as though she could not bear to touch her. Under her breath she said:

"Sonia, I'll never forgive you for this . . . never!"

"I don't care!"

"But you will," interrupted Jane, "because if you don't control yourself this instant I shall go straight upstairs and tell Uncle John everything."

That brought Sonia to her senses. Panting, wild-eyed, she stared at Jane, then began to whimper.

"Well, it's true. Why shouldn't I say it? Jane . . ."

"I don't want to talk to you," broke in Jane. "I think you're off your head. And I'm sorry for any help I've ever given you."

Sonia flung up her arms with a dramatic gesture of despair. The black lace mantilla slipped from her head. She caught it in her hand and turning, rushed speechlessly up the stairs to her own room.

Jane stood motionless. She felt quite sick. It wasn't so much that she resented what Sonia had said. She was not ashamed of loving Pat. But to have the thing screamed aloud . . . her well-guarded secret exposed in that way, possibly to *him* . . . that was unbearable!

In a dazed way she looked at the fountain-pen in her hand and remembered that her uncle was waiting for her to go back with some ink. She was not by nature melodramatic or hysterical like Sonia. When there was something to be done she did it, no matter how unpleasant. If she had to face Pat in that lounge she would face him. The ink was there, on the one and only writing desk. She had seen it. She only hoped desperately that Pat had *not* heard.

Then the striped curtains parted. Pat walked through

and they came face to face. He had, of course, been an unwilling listener to the scene which Sonia had made. He, too, was white, and there was a sick look in his eyes. His gaze met and held Jane's for an instant. Then, to her dismay, a burning tell-tale flush spread over her face and throat. She could not speak. She walked straight past him into the lounge.

He looked after her, his emotions chaotic. But he was more conscious of shame than anything else in this hour. Shame at Sonia's treachery to the cousin who had always been so loyal to her.

He knew that to-night's events had torn the last roots of infatuation from his heart. In a way it was a relief, because he could not suffer about Sonia any more. He could not even hate her. He only felt indifferent. And indifference is the final nail in the coffin of love.

He would like to have said something to Jane, tried to have helped her, make things easier for her. He knew perfectly well what agonies of embarrassment and humiliation she must be enduring. She, who was so proud. She was the last girl in the world to want any man to know that she cared for him under such conditions as these. And it had never entered his head until Sonia's words had put it there, that Jane was in love with him. She had been a fine friend, and a hard critic. But he had never suspected that she entertained more intimate feelings for him.

He might have doubted the truth of what Sonia had said had it not been for that burning revealing colour on Jane's face just now. That had betrayed her. For an instant he put a hand up to his eyes. God! What a mess! But whatever he did in the future he must try not to let her see that he *knew*. He was so grateful to her for all that she had done for him. He owed her so much. And he felt so completely unworthy of her love, if indeed, she had honoured him with it.

Jane came through with the ink. They avoided looking at each other this time. But Pat said, with a deliberate attempt at casualness:

"What's our Jane doing snooping round with pen and ink and that determined expression? On business bent for the Chief?"

"Yes. We're working. You're the one that's snooping round."

She passed him, her heart-beats hurting her, dark lashes hiding the distress in her eyes. As she reached the staircase, Pat threw a swift, unhappy look at her back.

"Good night, Jane."

"Good night," she said, without looking round, and went upstairs and passed out of sight.

She was more wretched than she had ever been in her life. Pat's casual treatment of her downstairs just now had raised a doubt in her mind as to whether he *had* heard what Sonia had said. There was no definite need for her to feel quite so outraged or ashamed. But she did and she was *miserable*.

It would be a good thing, she thought bitterly, when this trip ended. There seemed no hope now of happiness or peace for any of them. As far as she could see, tomorrow's advance into the wilderness, where they would be flung more than ever upon each other's company, would be sheer purgatory. And she dreaded it.

CHAPTER SEVENTEEN

It was, as Jane had anticipated, another sleepless night. Sonia shared a double room with her and spent most of the night crying from sheer self-pity. And then when Jane was at last allowed to go to sleep, her rest was curtailed by the early and unexpected appearance of Mr. Royale. He came into their room in his dressing-gown, his genial face downcast.

"Rather unfortunate news, you girls," he said. "We shan't be able to leave the hotel this morning. Our chauffeur's indisposed."

Sonia said nothing. As far as she was concerned Pat could be ill and stay so. Her humiliation last night at his hands had been so complete that she almost hated him.

But Jane rubbed her tired eyes and was immediately anxious on Pat's behalf.

"What's wrong with him, Uncle John?"

Mr. Royale thought it was a touch of 'flu. At any rate Connel had sent a message to him this morning and asked him to go along and see him. He had found the young man looking pretty cheap, had taken his temperature— Mr. Royale always carried a thermometer—and it was well up. Pat also complained of headache and pains, which had come on suddenly in the night. He was covered with confusion and full of apologies, but thought it unwise to tackle the day's journey.

"To which I agreed," finished Mr. Royale. "Of course he must stay in bed. No doubt he'll be all right in the morning."

When breakfast was over Jane went along to Pat's room. In answer to her knock a voice said: *"Entrada."*

She walked in. The curtains were drawn. In the shadows Pat lay in bed, shivering with fever under a thin blanket.

He looked at Jane with over-bright eyes and groaned.

"Oh, so it's you! Welcome, Jane. I thought it was that greasy, fat, unattractive woman who calls herself the chambermaid."

Jane walked to the bedside.

"Never you mind about attractive women. You just hurry up and get well," she said in her brusque way, but her brown eyes were soft and anxious for him.

He blinked at her.

"I feel like hell, Jane Daunt. Can't think what's wrong. Came on so suddenly in the night."

"It's a visitation on you for your sins. Have you taken some aspirin?"

"One."

"Ridiculous. You want three at least. I'll crush some and get you some warm milk.

Pat groaned again and turned his back on her.

"Warm milk! Sure, and I'd be sick as a dog. Jane— don't start bullying me when I'm ill."

She looked at the black tousled head on the white pillow . . . such a darling boyish head, she thought. And she loved him so frightfully! But she kept up her stern demeanour, made one or to practical suggestions, carried them out, and then left him, promising to look at him again later.

She joined her uncle and cousin, who were down in the lounge.

"Well, what do you think of him?" asked Mr. Royale.

"He looks rotten," said Jane. "But I don't suppose it's anything but 'flu."

"Get a doctor," said Sonia pettishly.

"My dear!" expostulated her father, "there won't be an English doctor in Pogador. A Spanish 'medico', perhaps, but you might as well consign yourself to the grave straight away as send for one of them."

"A nice place you've brought us to, Daddy."

"Come, come, Babe. Look at the sunshine, and that glorious collection of palm trees out there. You've got your tail down for some reason or other. Not sickening for 'flu too, are you, darling?"

"No," said Sonia, and lapsed into sullen silence.

The three of them spent the morning inspecting the fine old architecture in the Arab quarter of Pogador. Mr. Royale enjoyed himself. He did not mind the delay. Jane took notes diligently, but Sonia was bored and had little to say. She was not amused by the bazaars. She was never really amused unless she was being the centre of interest herself, or some attractive man was making love to her. Now that she had lost Pat she had lost all interest in this holiday. The relationship between herself and Jane was strained, too. She had said more than she intended last night and she knew that Jane was angry with her.

But there was more trouble in store for the Royale party than any of them had bargained for. When they reached the hotel they found it in chaos. The servants were tearing about with scared faces and the stout black-bearded gentleman in the red fez who called himself the manager, immediately rushed to Mr. Royale and began to babble incoherently.

The two girls stared at each other.

"What's he saying?" demanded Sonia.

"I don't know," said Mr. Royale. "It's all in Spanish, and I can't understand when they speak at that speed. Something has happened, anyhow. The whole place seems to be fermenting. Jane, my dear, run up and see if Connel's any better, and if he knows what the trouble is. He's our only interpreter."

Jane started to walk across the hall, but there was no

need for her to go farther. Pat, himself, appeared. He was in pyjamas and dressing-gown. He was hollow-eyed and his cheeks were scarlet with fever.

"What on earth are you doing out of bed?" cried Jane.

Pat was shivering visibly.

"Have you heard?" he said.

"Heard what?" asked Mr. Royale. "What the deuce is all this about, Connel? Everybody's tearing about like a lot of lunatics."

"They're packing up to get out, sir. In about half an hour there won't be a soul left in this place."

"But why? What's happened?"

And then Pat's lips formed and uttered the dreaded word . . . just one small word, but sufficient to make the faces of his listeners blanch.

"*Smallpox*," he said.

Sonia immediately screamed.

"*Oh!*" and her hands flew up to her delicate pink-and-white cheeks as though, in an instant, she visualised her loveliness being destroyed by that most dreaded scourge of the East.

Mr. Royale said:

"Good God!"

Jane stood still, her gaze fixed on Pat.

No word came from her. Following instantly upon the shock of what Pat had said there came to her the fearful suspicion:

"*Pat . . . has he got it?*"

Pat was telling the Chief what he knew.

During the morning nobody had been near him, in spite of the fact that he had rung his bell constantly. Then he got up and walked into the corridor and saw the Algerian who had waited on them last night, carrying a bundle of clothes down the stairs. He had questioned the fellow, who had told him that four of the staff had gone down suddenly with smallpox. Nobody intended to stay except a kitchen-boy and an old Arab who washed dishes, both of whom had had the disease.

"But they can't abandon the hotel," protested Mr. Royale. "It's preposterous."

"They're a lot of cowards," said Pat. "And it's just what they will do."

"Well, whoever wants to stay in it?" said Sonia in a high-pitched voice. "We must get away ourselves at once —at once!"

"Of course," said her father. "I ought never to have brought you here, but it never entered my head that there'd be an outbreak like this . . . it's terrible, terrible!"

Then Jane, whose dark eyes had never wavered from Pat's feverish face, said sharply:

"But what about Connel? He can't travel. He's in a high temperature. He might get pneumonia."

"I'll be all right," said Pat.

But even as he spoke he felt deadly faint and swayed on his feet.

Jane dropped a parcel which she had bought in the bazaar that morning, sprang to his side and put a supporting arm around him.

"No . . . you're far from all right!"

Sonia clutched her father's arm.

"Daddy . . . *daddy* . . . *he's* probably got it."

Mr. Royale's cheeks lost all their healthy colour.

"My dear . . . what an idea. . . ."

"But it may be true!" panted Sonia. "It probably is. Jane, come away from him, don't touch him!"

Jane threw her a look of withering contempt.

"What shall I do . . . just let him drop?"

"But, my dear, if he has got it . . ." began her uncle.

"Well, if he has, he isn't going to be left to it like an animal on a bundle of straw, is he?" Jane asked furiously.

Pat only half-heard the little storm which was raging over his head. All the faces, the Chief's, Sonia's, Jane's, were revolving round him. The pain in his head was excruciating. But he was conscious of Jane's protective arm, of her defending voice, and he knew suddenly that she *did* love him and that it was love in the real sense of the word.

He laughed stupidly, swaying on his feet.

"Sonia's wise . . . not to touch me . . . mustn't risk anything . . . but I . . . I haven't got it . . . only vaccinated . . . little while ago. . . ."

Then the world blacked out and he went down like a stone at Jane's feet, almost dragging her with him.

Sonia refused to let go of her father's arm.

"Daddy, don't touch him, you mustn't. Let Jane be a fool if she wants."

"What in God's name shall we do?" said Mr. Royale weakly. "We were wrong, very wrong, Babe, not to be vaccinated before we came out to Morocco. I shall never forgive myself if I've brought you into danger."

"We must go away at once!" said Sonia.

"Sonia's right, Jane. We must get out of this immediately and drive straight back to Tangier."

"And take Pat with us?" asked Jane, looking up, the Christian name slipping unconsciously from her lips.

"That's impossible," said Sonia. She was trembling with fright. "If he's got it, we'll all get it. We daren't risk that."

"Very well," said Jane. "If he stays here I stay with him."

"My dear Jane—" began Mr. Royale.

"It's unthinkable that we should all leave him here to die if he is really ill," cut in Jane. "You can see for yourself that these rats are all leaving the sinking ship and soon there won't be a soul in the hotel. I can't let Pat lie here and starve. He ought to be in bed now. Uncle John, you must help me carry him in to the divan in the lounge. We can drag him there between us and I'll get some blankets from upstairs."

"It isn't fair to make Daddy touch him . . ." began Sonia.

Then Jane turned on her.

"Oh—you make me sick. And after all . . ."

She choked and paused. She was going to say: "After all your protestation of loving him. . . ." But she dared not give Sonia away in front of her father.

Sonia was thinking of nothing but that awful word *smallpox*. In her estimation it was not the time for romance, or for remembering that she had ever been in love with Pat. She looked at his unconscious figure with horror, all her anxiety for herself.

Mr. Royale, in a state of nerves and slightly dazed by the whole thing, allowed his niece to take command of the situation. It seemed to him a critical one and there was no time for him to wonder why Jane should be so concerned about young Connel. He just did what she asked. Together they managed to drag Pat into the Moorish lounge and got him on to the divan. Jane tore upstairs and came down again with blankets, which she piled over the sick man. Then, with a white set face, she faced her uncle and cousin.

"Now listen," she said, "there's no time to argue or dither. Pat's very ill. He says that he was only vaccinated the other day so I don't suppose he's got smallpox, and *I'm* not going to worry. I was vaccinated myself not so many years ago. The main thing is that he mustn't be moved at the moment. Drive him out in the car now and he'll certainly get pneumonia and die. But you two have got to get away. Uncle John, you must take the Victor and drive back to Tangier. You won't get there till midnight, but it's the only thing to do. Then you can send an ambulance out from the clinic for Pat. I'll stay here and nurse him until you come. It's only a question of twenty-four hours."

"My dear, it's very noble—" began Mr. Royale.

"It's nothing of the kind," she interrupted. "I want to do it. But you and Sonia mustn't stay."

Mr. Royale turned helplessly to his daughter.

She took his arm and clung to it, avoiding Jane's clear stern gaze.

"Yes, Daddy, Jane's right. Let's get off quickly. It doesn't matter about food. We daren't touch any food from this place. Oh, *come on*, quickly . . . they can bring our luggage back in the ambulance. Don't let's wait for it."

For an instant Mr. Royale hesitated. He eyed his niece with misgiving.

"I don't feel I should leave you, my dear. . . ."

Jane, wasting no time, was crushing some aspirin in a slip of white paper.

"I shall be quite all right, Uncle John. And the sooner you reach Tangier, the sooner we'll have help."

"God bless you, my dear," said Mr. Royale, with the suspicion of a break in his voice. "You're like your mother was before you . . . a very brave woman."

Jane shook her head and smiled. Uncle John didn't understand. It wasn't brave to stay behind with the man you loved, and face danger with him. She would have had to have much more courage to leave Pat lying here alone.

She went out into the sunlit street and saw them off. Sonia, now in the car, was still jittering, but bade Jane good-bye and was seized with sudden remorse at the sight of her small solitary figure standing there on the doorstep.

"Will you be all right, Janie? Hadn't you better come with us?"

"No," said Jane coldly.

"Don't think too badly of me, Jane. I know I'm a coward ... but *smallpox*."

"We don't know that he's got it yet," snapped Jane. "Good-bye."

CHAPTER EIGHTEEN

A FEW moments later Jane watched the big shining Victor disappear in a cloud of dust. Perhaps then her heart quailed a very little. Uncle John had gone ... and she was alone with a very sick man in a practically deserted hotel, in an isolated Moorish town full of thieving natives and the lowest type of Spaniard. Not pleasant! Then the thought of Pat and her love for him overwhelmed her and cast out all fear.

Quickly she went back into the lounge. Pat's eyes were wide open now and he was muttering under his breath and obviously delirious. She took his hot hand and held it a moment, looking anxiously down at him. She had no particular knowledge of nursing, only practical commonsense and that mother instinct which is in every woman who loves. She could only do what she thought best. She had not the slightest idea how long smallpox took to develop or what the symptoms would be. But somehow she did not think that Pat had got it. They might, of course, both catch it just through staying here, but there was no alternative.

She decided that it would be wise to try and get hold of the local "medico". At least he would know how to deal with the illnesses of his own country. She found her pocket-dictionary and prepared a question in Spanish, and then tried to find somebody who would listen to her.

The manager himself had seized his things and departed. He did not intend to risk anything. Jane, wandering from room to room, found nobody in the hotel except the old Arab and the boy in the kitchen. She tried to make them understand what she wanted. But it was hopeless. They were both willing and eager to help her, but could do nothing but look at her like uncomprehending animals, roll their eyes, gesticulate, and pour torrents of bastard Spanish and Arabic into her ears.

The kitchen was in chaos. The cooks had departed in the middle of preparing the midday meal. Jane, although she was healthily hungry, decided that she would not eat any of the food, in case it was infected. She must go hungry for twenty-four hours. And it would not matter if Pat had nothing to-day but drinks. She found a saucepan, poured some water into it, boiled it and took it upstairs to the lounge. She could give Pat sips of that when it cooled down.

Pat tossed and moaned and muttered on his pillows. Jane left him again and hurried out into the street. The little square was deserted. Pogador appeared to give no sign of life. The rabbits had scuttled into their warrens. A rumour had been spread by an ignorant member of the hotel staff that the English chauffeur had brought a mysterious plague to Pogador . . . an illness resulting in rapid death. Already two of the hotel servants had succumbed, not from smallpox, the tale-bearer said, but this plague. The English gentleman and the golden-haired *señorita* had already fled from the town in their car. Nobody, therefore, would go near the hotel. Smallpox was bad enough, but the thought of an unknown plague spread terror through the superstitious natives in all quarters.

When Jane appeared, anybody that saw her scuttled away from her, believing her also to be a carrier of the fatal malady.

She found it hopeless to try to approach anybody or to find the medical man. So at length she returned to the abandoned hotel and to Pat's side.

She sat down beside him, wiped her burning face with a handkerchief and closed her eyes. Heavens! she was tired and hot. This was a bad business and quite frankly she could not look forward to the long hours in front of her. Hours of anxiety over Pat's condition and without food for herself, without even daring to make herself a cup of tea down in that filthy kitchen.

Pat threw up an arm and moaned.

"Sonia!"

Jane's lips tightened. So he was still thinking of *her* . . . Sonia who would have abandoned him to his fate this day! Not very jolly for her to sit here and listen to him raving about another woman.

Then Pat looked straight at her with his glazed eyes and muttered.

"You're vile . . . you're *vile* . . . !"

Jane laid a hand on his forehead and stroked back the thick dark hair.

"You're not talking to me, I hope," she said, with a flash of her old humour.

"Go away," said Pat. "Don't try and get me back this way, Sonia. Despicable . . . hate you. . . ."

Jane lifted her brows. So that was how he felt about Sonia! Well, it wasn't anything for her to be jealous of! She went on smoothing his forehead. He thrust her away and babbled about his love and his hate.

She went upstairs to her bedroom and brought down a bowl of cold water, a sponge, and towel. The only thing that she could do was to bathe him and try to lower his temperature. So she tucked up her sleeves and set to work on him in her practical way. He moved fretfully under her touch, but she managed to cool him down a little, wiping him carefully with a towel, like a mother with a sick child.

An hour or two passed. Pat grew delirious again, and she gave him some of the boiled water which had grown cool. He gulped it thirstily and then lay back on the cushions, gasping.

"Lie still," she begged. "Lie still and try to sleep."

Pat stared up at her without consciousness.

"Devil," he said through his teeth.

She gave a weak laugh.

"My dear Pat . . ."

"Cruel as hell," he said, and putting up an arm suddenly, caught her slim, small body and pulled her down against him.

"I loved you once," he muttered. "I adored you . . . believed in you. . . ."

Jane struggled in his hold. Her whole body was hot and resentful because she knew that to him she was Sonia, the phantom of his sick ravings.

"Stop that, Pat. Let me go."

He covered her hair with wild kisses.

"You're so lovely . . . so sweet. . . ."

"Let me go, I tell you . . ." said Jane.

She made desperate efforts to get away from him, but in his delirium he was too strong for her and suddenly she felt sick and faint. She struggled no more but lay still, her face buried against his shoulder. He, too, was quiet. For a moment Jane could think of nothing except her hopeless love for this man. The tears sprang to her eyes and scorched her burning face. But she thought:

"I wish I could die . . . like this . . . with him!"

Pat's eyes shut as though he were asleep. For a time

165

neither of them stirred. At length some of the rolling mists cleared from the sick man's brain and he grew suddenly aware of real things. His lashes lifted, saw, hazily, the striped silk curtains and mosaic walls of the Moorish lounge; became conscious of the divan on which he was lying, and conscious, too, that a girl . . . a slim girl was lying in the crook of his arm crying as though her heart would break.

For a few moments, weak and dizzy, he made neither movement nor did he speak. But he looked stupidly at the girl's dark ruffled head and her prostrate figure in the thin blue linen dress, beside him. Then he knew who it was. With a sense of shock he spoke her name.

"*Jane!*"

Instantly she drew away from him and sprang to her feet. Gasping, drawing a hand across her wet eyes like an ashamed boy, she looked down at him.

"Jane," he whispered again. "What the devil . . .?"

"So you're sane again," she broke in.

He knit his brows.

"Sane? What's been happening? What am I doing here? And why were you . . ."

She interrupted him, her cheeks scorching with embarrassment.

"You were delirious. Old idiot, you pulled me down and I couldn't get away . . . raving you were!"

He looked up at her, growing every instant clearer and more fully conscious of things. And very conscious indeed of the memory of Jane lying there sobbing beside him.

"My dear," he said. "Why were you crying?"

"I wasn't!" she said angrily. "And don't talk. You've got to lie quiet. You've been like a madman with fever, but I suppose the aspirin's done the trick. I bunged about half the bottle into you, trying to get your temperature down. I gave you a sponge bath as good as any hospital nurse, too. Here . . . drink some of this. . . ."

She picked up a cup, knelt beside him, and raised it to his lips.

He sipped the water gratefully.

"Thanks, Jane. But sure and I don't understand . . . what's the matter . . . where's everybody?"

Before she could answer remembrance flashed back into his mind. A look of horror came into his eyes.

"Good God . . . *the smallpox*. . . !"

"Oh, do be quiet, Pat. You aren't fit to talk."

"But, Jane," he gasped. "Jane, you oughtn't to be here . . . I might have it. . . ."

"You said you've been vaccinated."

"So I have, but there's a risk."

"I don't think so. I was vaccinated, too. But Sonia wasn't, and she and Uncle John have gone back to Tangier. They'll send an ambulance out from the clinic for you."

"Good God!" he said again. "They left you here?"

"They had to. I wanted to stay."

He lay still, breathing quickly. He wished he did not feel so sick and weak. But he looked at Jane speechless with gratitude. It seemed to him the most wonderful thing in the world that she should have volunteered to stay and take such an appalling risk, no matter how slender the chances of either of them being stricken down. Jane felt suddenly shy of that look in his eyes and turned away from it.

"I'm not worrying," she said briskly.

"But I am," he whispered. "For you . . . you oughtn't to have stayed . . . I can never thank you. . . ."

"There's nothing to thank me for. I only want you to be quiet."

"I will be, Jane, but tell me . . . who else is in the hotel?"

She gave a nervous little laugh.

"Only us, as far as I can see. But what's it matter? We wouldn't dare eat the food even if it was served to us. Anyway it's best for you to keep on water, and I shan't starve. It's all good for the slimming."

"What time is it?"

"About four. Uncle John won't get to Tangier much before midnight because he drives slower than you do. And then if they send the ambulance out straight away it should reach us by ten or eleven to-morrow morning. It isn't so bad."

He lay still again. He had never known anything finer than this girl's pluck. He said huskily:

"Why didn't you go with them? God, Jane, it was swell of you, but you shouldn't . . ."

"Don't say any more. Go to sleep."

"I've been a nice fool, playing this trick on you all, but I think I know what it is. It's a touch of the sun. It affects me that way sometimes. I did this on my father when I was a boy, when we were in Morocco. My temperature plays odd games with me and flies up sky-high for nothing. That's what it is . . . a touch of the sun."

Her heart went out to him in a great rush. Dear God, that was all that mattered to her, to know that there was nothing more wrong with him than that. Out of sheer weakness the tears came into her eyes again and rolled down her cheeks.

"That's grand, Pat."

"*You're* grand," he said. "And Jane, I'm damned sorry if I did or said anything rotten, just now . . . when I was delirious . . . I made you cry . . . and now you're crying again . . . Jane, mavourneen. . . ."

She choked back a sob fiercely. She *would not* make a

fool of herself just because she had been through a trying time and her nerves were frayed and her emotions all stirred. But when Pat said "mavourneen" in that devastating voice of his, what was any girl to do . . . any girl who loved him?

"For heaven's sake stop talking and go to sleep," she gasped through her sobs, and terrified of herself, rushed out of the lounge and up to her bedroom.

When she came back to Pat she had herself well in control again. She had taken off her dress, which had been badly crumpled by the tussle with Pat, and put on a dressing-gown of orange Turkish towelling, tied with a cord round the waist. She used it for sea-bathing, as a rule, and as it had sleeves only to the elbows, it was quite a cool thing to wear. It also seemed to her a practical garment in which to nurse Pat. If his temperature went up later on, she would probably have to sluice him down again.

The swift Eastern darkness fell upon them. While it was yet light Jane had taken the precaution of finding a lamp and some matches, for there was no other form of illumination in this primitive hotel. She also had a queer feeling against leaving the place open all night, and so she went firmly round the hotel and shut and barred all the doors. She had no wish to be set upon by a band of desperadoes from the mountains, or some thieving natives of the town who were willing to risk "the plague" for what valuables there were to steal. And by now she knew that she and Pat were utterly alone. The stricken servants lay in their quarters, which were in a separate building through a courtyard. And the old Arab and the kitchen-boy had abandoned their posts.

Pat slept on, for which Jane was profoundly thankful, for it showed an improvement in his condition. By now she was terribly hungry. She had boiled some more water and drank plenty of that, but the long day without any nourishment was beginning to tell on her. Also her nerve was shaken. She sat close to Pat's side, huddled in a chair with a blanket over her knees, for it was growing cold now that the sun had set. The single oil lamp shed an eerie light in the Oriental lounge and flung strange shadows against the walls. It was quiet, much too quiet. An almost uncanny silence brooded over Pogador. The only sound to be heard was the distant throb of drums and the thin wail of some Eastern instrument from the native quarter. That in itself made sinister hearing.

The worst of Jane's troubles was that she had run out of cigarettes. She needed one badly to calm her nerves just now. Her eyelids grew hot and heavy. She longed for sleep, but dared not close her eyes. Somebody might break open a window or get into the hotel. She must keep guard over her patient. After that high fever he would be very weak and unable to protect himself.

Of course, she was just being a nervous little idiot, she told herself. Nobody was likely to come near this place to-night. And to-morrow help would come from Tangier.

But supposing her uncle and cousin never reached Tangier? Dear old Uncle John was so unintelligent about motor mechanism, and if there was a breakdown he would never be able to put things right. He would have to wait for help. A delay like that and it would perhaps mean forty-eight hours before they could send the ambulance to Pogador.

Pat awoke about half-past eleven. Jane gave a little sigh of relief as he opened his eyes. These chill, dark hours, huddled up in her chair, trying to keep awake, had seemed unending.

She lifted the cup of water to his lips, supporting him with an arm.

"Feeling better?"

"M'm," he said drowsily.

She put her fingers on his pulse. It seemed to her a good deal slower. His eyes looked sunken, but there was no longer that hectic flush on his cheeks.

"You *are* better, I believe," she said. "Let's take your temperature."

She could have wept with joy to find that it was just below 100°. Earlier in the day it had been over 103°. She took the thermometer and smiled at him.

"It's well down. You're all right, Pat. I think you're right about the sunstroke. That's all it is. If it had been the *other* you'd have had all sorts of horrid symptoms by now."

He stretched his arms above his head, yawned, and looked round at the lamp-lit lounge.

"Gosh! I feel I've been asleep for years. What have you been doing?"

"Just sitting here."

He looked at the slim young figure in the orange dressing-gown and became aware of the pallor and tension in her face. And he realised suddenly what a strain she had been through.

"Aren't you a marvel," he said. "Just a marvel!"

Jane blushed, and immediately snapped:

"Rot!"

"And are we still ship-wrecked, so to speak, on a desert island?"

"We are. Not a soul in the hotel. I went round before dark. I thought it better to shut ourselves in."

"Much better," he agreed. "Is it late?"

"Getting on for twelve."

"Have you had any sleep?"

"I don't want any."

"That's rubbish. You've been watching me. I'm all

171

right now. You go to sleep now—wrap yourself up on that other sofa over there."

"No, *you* should sleep again."

"I don't want to."

"Pat, you're weak as a rat, and whatever you've got, it's important for you to sleep."

He fixed his blue heavy eyes upon her.

"Do you never think of yourself?"

"Certainly. But I'm not tired. And you're my patient, and you've got to do what the nurse says."

"What a grand nurse she is, too."

Suddenly her head lifted and her eyes widened.

"Listen!"

"What to?"

She didn't answer for a moment. Then she walked to the striped curtains and parted them. After a pause she let them fall again and turned back to him with a half-shamed laugh.

"It's nothing. I just thought I heard . . ."

"You've got the jimjams," he broke in. "And I don't wonder. It's all been an awful strain on you. You're tired out. You've got to sleep now, Jane, and if there's anything to listen for, I'll do the listening for the next few hours."

She walked back to his bedside and was furious with herself because the tears welled into her eyes. She was weak from lack of food, and after the heat, exertion and tension of the day. He saw those tears glittering on her lashes and was filled with indescribable tenderness for her. Until now he had felt too ill to think much about her, but in this hour the full realisation of her courage and what she had done for him came upon him. He held out a hand.

"Come here, Jane."

She obeyed, and found herself placing her fingers in his.

"Now, Pat, be good and sleep again," she began, and made an effort to blink back those tears which she felt were ridiculous.

He said:

"I want to tell you that I think you're the grandest girl I've ever known. Not one in a thousand would have risked smallpox like this. I wish to God I thought I could do something to repay you. If I grow to be a million I shall never forget that you stayed behind in this infernal place with me."

She shook her head mutely, and stood there speechlessly with her hand locked in his. And the sight of Jane Daunt, who had always been so practical, so poised, so cool, looking like a child in her dressing-gown, with her dark, ruffled hair and with those tears streaming down her cheeks, was infinitely moving to him. It was impossible for him not to remember what he had heard last night . . . remember that Sonia had accused Jane of being in love with him. Well, what more could any woman have done for any man, than Jane had done for him this day? And how in God's name was he ever going to repay such a debt?

Suddenly he drew her hand against his cheeks with a caressing movement and then kissed it.

"The grandest girl I've ever known," he repeated. "Thank you, dear, and . . . bless you!"

It took Jane her last ounce of pride and pluck to withstand that stirring tenderness from him. She could so easily have broken down and flung herself straight into his arms. But somehow she managed to laugh helplessly, drag her fingers away and say:

"I'm just the world's idiot. Don't mind me, Pat. It's the diet. I don't think slimming agrees with me."

Then she went back to the chair and drew the blanket firmly round her.

"A few more hours of sleep and you'll be a different man," she added. "And in the morning . . . sing hey for the rescue party!"

"You're an obstinate child," he said. "But I'm obstinate, too, and I am *not* going to sleep until you've had some rest. I can't really think why we don't both go to sleep."

Jane blew her small nose violently.

"Just in case of robbers and thieves."

"Well, I daresay we'll wake up if they come, and as long as they leave us alone they're welcome to take anything they see."

"Quite," said Jane with a laugh that had a break in it.

"Well, I'll make a bargain. I'll go to sleep if you do."

She agreed to that. And once her heavy eyelids closed she was soon fast asleep because she was really worn out. But Pat had no intention of sleeping. It was he who watched over her during the rest of that sinister night, and during that silent watch, the knowledge came to him that all these weeks and months he had been a blind fool. Jane had loved him and he had loved Sonia. And therein he had made the biggest mistake of his life. For it was Jane Daunt and not Sonia who was worth a man's loving, and for Jane, with her grand character and that adorable mixture that was in her of soft femininity and courageous boy, who could fashion the ladder on which a man might indeed, climb to the stars!

CHAPTER NINETEEN

HAD Jane and Pat sat down and thought about it, they might have named a dozen people who would come to their rescue; authorities of the English clinic in Tangier heading the list. But never would they have hit upon the person who was eventually responsible for putting an end to that nightmare scare in Pogador.

Soon after dawn broke over the Moorish town, flushing the white minarets and shuttered houses with rose and opalescent light, a little bus rattled over the cobbled street and pulled up in the square. It was the fortnightly bus from Tetuan, and Pogador's one method of communication with the outer world.

Out of this bus stepped two or three superior Arab merchants, a dark-skinned soldier of the Foreign Legion the driver with his mail bag, and—a slim, blue-eyed man —who might be English or American—who wore a check suit and a black beret at a rakish angle on his fair head.

He was not surprised by the deserted appearance of the square, for it was still very early in the morning. He found the main entrance barred, and knocked upon it loudly. They should be open to meet the bus, he thought crossly, and stood there in the fresh cool morning yawning and stretching his limbs.

Nobody answered his summons. He knocked again loudly and called in Spanish.

"*Oiga! Dega!*"

It was that call which roused Jane from her slumbers. She started up violently. The little lounge was still dim, for the sunlight had not penetrated through the thick curtains. She looked down at Pat. He was awake and had raised himself on one elbow.

"Somebody at the door. It can't be . . ."

"Not our rescue party, no—" she broke in. "They've scarcely had time to get back from Tangier. It's only five o'clock in the morning."

Fresh banging and roaring at the barred door. An explosive voice making demands in French, Spanish, and English. And it was at the sound of the English that Jane leapt to the door.

"Pat, listen. It'll be help of some kind, anyhow!"

With a fast-beating heart, Jane unbarred the front door of the hotel and flung it open. And the next moment she found herself staring, stupefied, at the fair-haired man in the beret.

"*Maurice!*" she gasped.

Maurice Gardener stared back at her. His face was a study in bewilderment, as he took in the sight of the small girlish figure in the orange dressing-gown, the ruffled hair, and pale little face. Then he took off his beret, blinking hard.

"*Mon Dieu!* Cousin Jane! Am I mad, or is it you?"

At any other time than this Jane would not have been pleased to see Sonia's husband. But at the moment he seemed an angel in disguise, and she straightway began to cry with sheer relief from the nervous tension which she had passed through since yesterday. She sobbed:

"Oh, Maurice, but I'm glad to see you."

He came into the hall, shaking his head in bewilderment.

"But, Jane, what does this mean? Why the tears? Why have you opened the door to me? Is the place bewitched? Are there no servants. . . ?"

Jane tried to stop crying.

"No. Nobody. Everyone's gone . . . oh, where have you come from?"

"On the bus from Tetuan. When I left Tangier I went straight to Tetuan and was so bored I couldn't remain. I heard there was a night bus leaving for this outlandish spot. Someone told me it was worth seeing and that the mountain air would do me good, so along I came. And *sapristi*, what a journey!"

He broke off and stared at Jane.

"Why are you crying? Where is . . . Sonia?"

Out tumbled Jane's story. Maurice dropped his bag,

lit a cigarette, and listened in amazement. His face changed colour somewhat when the word "smallpox" fell from her lips. He clicked his tongue.

"But this is serious. You poor little thing! What an experience for you. Why in heaven's name didn't you go with Sonia and Mr. Royale?"

"Because," said Jane in a low voice, "I wouldn't leave ... Mr. Connel."

Maurice Gardener pulled his lips down in a grimace.

"The gentleman with the strong right arm, *hein*? But I thought my charming wife was interested in him."

"I'm afraid you finished all that, Maurice."

"Well, this is no time to discuss such things. Here I am, a solitary visitor to a stricken town, and your Mr. Connel ... has he the smallpox?"

"No, we are both convinced he has not. He had sun-stroke. But Sonia was afraid that it was the other thing, and anyhow his temperature was so high yesterday we dared not move him."

Maurice nodded.

"So like Sonia. She would risk nothing for anybody. But you, Cousin Jane, I have always had a great admiration for you. I'm not surprised you stayed behind."

"Oh, give me a cigarette," said Jane, in confusion. "I've been dying for one."

He handed her his case.

"And I'm dying for food."

"You're not likely to get that ... the infection...."

"My dear Jane, I have the honour to inform you that I am immune from this plague. I had smallpox as a boy in France. It means nothing to me."

"Then doubtless you'll find something in the kitchen. But you'll have to find it for yourself," said Jane, half-laughing, half-crying.

"I will," he said. "But obviously it is essential for you

and Mr. Connel to get away from this place. When do you expect the ambulance?"

"Not for hours. And anyhow we don't need it now. Pat's almost well again—only he's too weak to walk far."

Maurice reflected, biting his lips.

"Then get him dressed, Jane, and I will commandeer the bus."

"The *bus!*" repeated Jane.

"Why not? The driver is a Spaniard. I can tackle him. He expects to remain here until the afternoon, and I can get you and Mr. Connel halfway to Tangier, and we will probably meet the rescue party. I am a good driver—then I will return home with the bus. Much better to get you away at once, isn't it so?"

"It would be a terrific relief," she said. "And, Maurice, it would be wonderful of you...."

He bowed as she paused.

"It will be a pleasure to me to be of some use in this world. My existence is generally futile. You have said hard words to me, Cousin Jane, on one or two occasions, but perhaps maybe you will give me this chance to show you that I am still—a gentleman!"

Jane wiped her eyes. It was typical of Maurice to be showy and grandiloquent, but she knew that he was coming up to the scratch as far as he could do. She said huskily:

"Thanks, Maurice. You're a brick."

He bowed again.

"From *petite* Cousin Jane that is flattery indeed!" He went out into the sunlight, prepared to bribe the driver, commandeer the bus, and take charge of the situation. Jane rushed back to Pat and told him the surprising news.

"Good lord!" said Pat. "What a queer state of affairs

. . . Sonia's husband coming to the rescue. Decent of him, Jane—after I've knocked the fellow down, too!"

"I think he has a good side to him, Pat."

Suddenly he held out a hand to her.

"And you, you've got something in you, Jane, that would bring out the best in any man."

She clung to his hand for a moment, her tears falling again.

"Sorry . . . for being . . . so stupid . . . I think it's just lack of food."

He drew the small hand to his lips.

"As long as I live I shall remember that you risked sheer horror in order to stay behind and look after me, Jane. Dear, dear Jane!"

"Oh, don't say nice things to me . . . I'm really not in the right state of mind to stand it, Pat," she said, her face puckered and wet with tears. "I'm going upstairs to dress, and bring down your things. Then we must get you up. You do feel strong enough?"

"Sure . . . another twenty-four hours and I'll be myself again. I reckon it's been a bit of fright about nothing."

She nodded, smiling at him through her tears.

And an hour later they were on the road to Tangier in that badly sprung, draughty, rattling little bus. Maurice sat at the wheel in excellent spirits, between his lips a cigarette, which he removed only to utter imprecations against the steering and the gears, which were, he informed his passengers, of pre-historic design.

The passengers themselves sat on their hard seats fully conscious of the luck which had come to them in the shape of Maurice Gardener.

It was good to be away from that hotel and the sinister atmosphere, and much of the discomfort of the bus was mitigated by the cushions and rugs which they had brought with them. Jane, still in her rôle of nurse, had wrapped Pat in blankets and filled a hot-water bottle for his feet, determined that he should not catch cold after the fever. And Maurice had rummaged the kitchens and found tinned biscuits which they could eat without fear and which assuaged some of the pangs of hunger now assailing both patient and nurse.

A never-to-be-forgotten journey!

Jane had little to say. But now and then her soft brown eyes rested upon Pat with a tenderness which she could barely conceal and an immense thankfulness that there was no need to be anxious about his condition.

As for Pat, it was to Jane rather than the passing scenery that his gaze frequently wandered. Gallant Jane, before whom mentally he bent his knee.

As for Maurice Gardener, Pat could only regard the gay, insolent figure at the wheel with a feeling of friendliness. It didn't seem to matter at all that he was Sonia's husband, and that it was he who had shattered the romance which Pat had woven so wildly around her. That all seemed long ago, another life. This was a new life in which reality had replaced romance. And nothing was so real or so important as the friendship which Jane had given him and the love which she had proven up to the hilt.

The sun rose higher as they journeyed along retracing the road which they had taken only two days ago. Soon it grew so hot that Pat was able to dispense with his two layers of blankets and rugs and his hot-water bottle. But Jane fussed over him.

"You're not to catch cold," she kept saying.

He smiled at her and answered:

"All right nurse. I'll be good."

It was not an ambulance which met them two hours later on that remote, sun-baked mountain road. It was the Victor driven by Mr. Royale, with an elderly man wearing glasses seated beside him. Jane and Pat recognised the shining bonnet of the car long before they came alongside. Maurice pulled up with a jerk and Jane climbed down from the bus and ran to Mr. Royale.

"Uncle John!"

He looked at her with amazement. His face was pale and drawn and his eyes bloodshot. He was deadly tired.

"Good heavens!" he exclaimed. "What are you doing in *that*. . . ." he pointed to the queer little bus which had the names of "Tetuan" "Pogador" painted upon it.

Jane explained. She told her uncle all that had happened since yesterday.

"Pat hasn't got smallpox at all," she finished breathlessly. "And I don't seem to be developing it, either. But, oh, Uncle John, we were glad to see Maurice Gardener, I can tell you!"

Mr. Royale drew a hand across his eyes. He had been much more worried about his niece than he cared to admit, and very conscience-stricken at having left her behind him.

"Well, thank God for that!" he said. "It's been a business, I tell you, my dear! I couldn't get an ambulance, and the clinic won't accept smallpox suspects, but I eventually found this extremely kind friend . . ." he indicated the man beside him, ". . . Dr. Pollock. He has a villa in Tangier, and he volunteered to come with me."

Jane greeted the doctor, who said:

"I might as well get out and take a look at the patient."

Whereupon he moved from the Victor into the bus and sat down beside Pat.

"You must be exhausted, Uncle John" said Jane, looking compassionately at Mr. Royale's haggard face.

He wiped his forehead with a handkerchief.

"A bit played out, my dear. I'm too old for these excitements. As for writing a book on Morocco . . . I'd as

181

soon go home and never set eyes on the infernal country again. This night has taken the spirit of adventure from me, all right."

"I think it's encouraged one in me," said Jane, with a funny little smile.

Mr. Royale looked at the driver of the bus and shook his head.

"Fancy that fellow Gardener turning up! I've never liked him, but I suppose we owe him something for this."

"I think we do," said Jane.

"Have you had anything to eat?" her uncle asked, conscious now that Jane's face was pinched and hollow-eyed.

"Only biscuits," she confessed.

"Well, we've brought hot drinks in thermos flasks, and food," he said. "And before I drive a step farther I'm going to take a cushion and a rug and sleep."

"We might all do the same," said Jane.

Dr. Pollock emerged from the bus and approached them.

"Nothing much wrong with that young fellow except a touch of the sun," he said.

"And I don't think there's much wrong with me except hunger," said Jane.

"You're a lot of frauds," said Dr. Pollock. "But it's just as well you're out of Pogador. It's about the most un-civilised spot in Morocco."

There followed a strange picnic; all of them sitting in the bus. Pat, Jane, and Maurice Gardener drank hot coffee and ate hard-boiled eggs and bread-and-butter ravenously. Never had food tasted so good. Mr. Royale and the doctor joined in the repast, and they might all have been old, attached friends. This queer encounter had brought them in close contact. They found themselves exchanging stories and jokes, laughing helplessly, quarrelling gaily over the last crumb of food and the last drop of coffee.

And after that they slept . . . all of them, including Maurice.

"They'll be raising blue murder in Pogador if I get back late with their bus," he said, "but, *mon Dieu*, I must have my piece of rest as well."

Later, when the afternoon had grown cooler and Pat had been transferred into the Victor, Maurice prepared to make the homeward journey. Jane shook hands with him and said:

"You've been grand to us, Maurice. I'm going to tell Sonia."

He shrugged his shoulders and pulled the beret more rakishly on the side of his head.

"The charming Sonia has no use for me, and I haven't much for her now. She has played the coward in this game."

"One must make allowances for Sonia," said Jane.

"I shall do what she has wanted me to do for so long," he said. "I shall set her free. Good-bye, Cousin Jane. We are not likely to meet again."

Driving back to Tangier in the Victor, Mr. Royale said:

"Not such a bad chap after all, Gardener. Very decent of him to collect that old bus and bring you young people out here. I felt I ought to do something in return, so I told him to look us up next time he was in London."

Pat and Jane exchanged glances. They both knew, somehow, that Maurice Gardener was not likely to call at the Royale house in London.

And John Royale was never to know that it was Sonia's husband to whom he had extended that invitation, for the divorce which set Sonia free later in the year was so discreetly manœuvred that Mr. Royale remained in ignorance of it and of the whole of that disastrous folly which had almost ruined his daughter in Paris two years ago.

CHAPTER TWENTY

ABOUT a month later Jane Daunt sat in her accustomed place at her desk in the office of the big Royale showrooms in Piccadilly.

She had had a busy day. It was a fine May, and in London there was plenty of business doing in the car world.

Jane, tired and hot, wiped the nib of her pen, sat back in her chair, and lit a cigarette.

It was half-past four. An hour which she had been eagerly awaiting ever since she started work to-day. Pat was coming to see her. There was a letter in her bag from him received this morning, telling her to expect him at this time. He had been away on one of his usual jobs on behalf of the Royale motor company, and Jane had not seen him for a week. A very long week it had seemed, for ever since their return from abroad they had been in contact almost daily. If he didn't catch a glimpse of her here in the office he rang her up at home or took her out for a meal or a picture. Since their adventures in Morocco, and in particular that sinister night together in Pogador, there had existed between them a comradeship and understanding that had been infinitely satisfying to Jane. As far as she could see it had been equally satisfying to Pat.

He had been a changed man since his return to London. The wild, irresponsible, impulsive Irishman had given place to a steadier man; a man still ambitious and hard-working, but with a more fully developed sense of proportion, one who could put a true value on things and did not waste his days in dreaming.

She had heard from everybody in the firm that he had been working furiously, and her uncle had personally expressed himself "pleased with young Connel".

The break between Sonia and Pat was final and absolute. They had not even had to endure each other's company on the return journey from Tangier, because Sonia, once she got back to El Minza, removed herself from the little party. Pat was finished with her, therefore she was finished with him. She had had a letter from an old school friend in Majorca, inviting her to stay out there, and she accepted. She left her father and cousin, pleading as an excuse that the horrible adventure in Pogador had completely destroyed her nerve, and she would not go a mile farther in the car. So Mr. Royale packed her off by sea to Majorca and he, his niece, and Connel returned to England alone.

As far as Jane could judge, Pat had put the past behind him very thoroughly.

During the journey back to England, and in the days that followed, Jane was no longer forced to undergo the torture of seeing the man she loved interest himself in another woman. She might not count in his life except as a friend, as she wanted to, but at least she was spared the misery of watching him head straight for disaster.

Jane looked at her watch. A quarter-to-five. Pat was late. He was coming up from the West country. Probably he was jammed in a traffic block. It was awful driving in London these days, she thought, what with all the heavy vehicles, private cars, all the irritating signals, and the Belisha beacons.

Sonia was coming back from Majorca to-morrow. She had met a marvellous young man out there in whom she was interested, so she had told Jane in the last letter received.

Well, whatever future troubles assailed Sonia, next time Jane was determined not to be mixed up in them. It was quite obvious that Sonia could not be happy unless she had a lover and was satisfying her personal vanity, and equally obvious that no disaster would ever teach her a lesson. One day, no doubt, when she was free, she would marry again, and then some unfortunate man as her husband would have to try to control her.

A voice behind Jane said:

"Hullo!"

Jane, in the act of dusting her small nose and smoothing an unruly lock of hair, swivelled round in her chair.

"Oh! Hullo, Pat. It's you."

Pat Connel came into the office and shut the frosted-glass door behind him. He looked brown and well and was wearing the grey flannels in which Jane always liked him. His blue eyes were brilliant and his voice held a note of excitement as he said:

"Great news, little Jane! G-r-e-a-t news!"

Jane blinked up at him.

"My dear Pat, what's happened?"

He balanced himself on the edge of the desk and handed her his cigarette-case.

"First of all, how's Jane?"

"Fine. And what mischief are you up to, Pat Connel?"

"No mischief at all. Sure and I'm a hard-working devil these days, and you know it. I've just sold two Victors in Devon and Cornwall."

Her brown eyes rested on him with a softness which was for him alone. He was such a boy, this "hard-working devil", and she wished she was not in love with him and that she could just feel in a platonic way about him as he did about her.

"Well," she said. "Come on—out with the news."

"I had a long-distance call from our ma ager last night. He thought I'd like to know that I'd been p moted."

"Promoted!" repeated Jane. "What to?"

"Sales manager in France, little Jane. N just salesman in England, but *manager* of the Continental depôt. I hear the Chief was impressed by my nowledge of languages when we were abroad, and they'v offered me this job at a salary of one thousand pounds nd commission. Jane, it's *grand*."

She sat still. She wanted to congratulate him. It *was* grand . . . a big job, and it would satisfy quite a few of Pat's ambitions. But it was going to take him away from London . . . from her. With a sinking heart she said:

"How splendid, Pat. No wonder you're excited. I suppose it means you . . . will live in Paris."

"Of course. I love Paris, don't you?"

"Love it," she echoed.

"Won't you smoke?"

"No, thank you."

"And there's some talk of me going to Madrid later on, as well, and trying to interest the Spaniards in our cars."

"Madrid, eh?" said Jane.

Their eyes met. Her lashes lowered nervously, and he suddenly flushed under his tan. They were both remembering that first fatal night they had spent in Madrid, the night when Mr. Royale had found his "chauffeur" kissing his daughter and had dismissed him. That night when Jane had suffered agonies of mind only a shade worse than she suffered now when there was no Sonia, but she was still no more than Pat's friend.

Pat said:

"I'm to start in June—two weeks' time."

Jane drummed her fingers on her blotter.

"So we shan't be seeing much more of you here."

He did not answer for a moment. He looked at her bent dark head. All remembrance of the folly of Madrid and of his infatuation for Sonia Royale was wiped out by another memory . . . one which he regarded as almost sacred . . . a slim young figure in an orange dressing-gown huddled beside him in the shadows in a Moorish hotel lounge; a gallant young figure keeping guard over him . . . a very gallant girl who had stayed behind in a fever-stricken town to nurse him and had taken an appalling risk for him.

He had realised that night that she loved him. He realised this afternoon that he loved her. And he did not know what to say, he, who was usually so ready with speeches, with an Irishman's faculty for making love to a pretty woman. But this was different, this profound feeling which welled up in him for Jane Daunt and brought a lump to his throat.

She looked up at him, her eyes bright and rather hard.

"You'll have to write occasionally and tell me how you're getting on."

"Will you miss me, Jane?"

She blushed to the roots of her hair.

"What a conceited question!"

"Well, will you? Tell me."

"Certainly not."

"You mean you won't miss me?"

"Why should I?"

"You're hedging."

"Oh, don't be so silly, Pat."

"Perhaps I am silly," he said. "But I've a notion that I'm going to miss you . . . just like hell!"

Her heart raced.

"Oh, no you won't."

"But I will, Jane, because your friendship means so much to me."

"You'll make new friends . . . in Paris."

"Maybe. And fall in love with a gay Parisienne, eh?"

Jane met his gaze unflinchingly.

"I wouldn't be at all surprised."

"Well, I would," he said roughly, "because I don't like Frenchwomen. And I'm not likely to fall in love with anybody. I'm much too much in love with you."

That staggered Jane so completely that she could only stare up at him speechlessly, her face changing from red to white. Then she gasped:

"Pat!"

He seized both her hands and wrung them.

"But it's true, Jane, mavourneen. I'm hopelessly in love with you. And it isn't a light, frivolous sort of love, nor an infatuation. I just adore you. I've been at your feet ever since that night in Pogador. I knew then that you were the grandest girl in the world."

"But—how absurd!"

"You mean you don't believe me. You have doubts of me? You think I change my feelings easily and quickly? But you've got to try and understand that that experience with Sonia *was* only an experience which just took all the scales from my eyes and taught me facts. And you . . . you've taught me all that I ever want to know. You've been so good to me, Jane. I suppose it's too much for me to expect you to go on being good . . . to ask you to try to believe me when I tell you that I love you better than anyone, anything in the world."

She shook her head dumbly, her fingers trembling in his.

"I don't know what to believe," she said weakly.

"But you must. I couldn't go on if you didn't. And that job in Paris won't mean a thing to me unless you'll come with me, Jane."

"Come with you!" she repeated.

"Yes. Marry me and come and live with me in Paris, my dear. I feel I've got something to offer you. A good job and a good screw. Of course the Chief may chuck me out for daring to propose to his niece. But as you've told me in the past, I've got plenty of nerve. Jane, *darling*, won't you marry me?"

"I . . . I can't think."

"I'll go to the Chief to-night and ask permission."

"Certainly not!" cried Jane. "Uncle John has no say at all in my private affairs. I shall marry whom I choose."

"But supposing he chucks me out?"

"He won't. I won't let him."

Pat drew a deep breath.

"Then you mean you *will* marry me?"

"I suppose so," said Jane weakly. "I expect I'm mad as a hatter. But I must . . . I must come with you, Pat. I love you so much! Life doesn't mean a thing to me either, without you."

He pulled her out of the chair into his arms.

"You're too good for me, Jane, but if you'll take me as I am . . . there's nothing I won't do to justify your trust in me."

Her arms were about his neck, and her cheeks, wet with tears, pressed against his. She whispered:

"If you love me, that's enough."

"Ah, *you* know how to love, Jane, my dearest. Haven't you proved it . . . a dozen times? Jane, you must teach me something about it, too. I want to learn all over again. And I swear you won't have to pull me out of Moorish cafés, or lecture me . . ."

"More than once a year?" she finished for him, half-laughing, half-crying.

"Never," he said, smoothing the dark hair back from her forehead. "Never, my sweetheart, if I have you. You're so *very* sweet!"

190

An office boy opened the door and peered in; Jane, with Pat's lips upon hers, was not aware of the fact. The boy gave one look at the Chief's secretary and the young Irish salesman locked in each other's arms, then went out again, mischievously whistling: "Love in·Bloom."

THE END